Farewell Song

Farewell Song

Rabindranath Tagore

Translated by Radha Chakravarty

Hesperus Worldwide

Hesperus Worldwide
Published by Hesperus Press Limited
19 Bulstrode Street, London w1u 2jn
www.hesperuspress.com

Farewell Song first published in Bengali as Shesher Kabita in 1928
First published by Penguin India, 2011
This edition published by Hesperus Press Limited, 2011

Designed and typeset by Fraser Muggeridge studio
Printed in Jordan by Jordan National Press

ISBN: 978-1-84391-858-5

Contents

to my son Abhishek,
the poet in the family

Introduction

Shesher Kabita was written in 1928 and serialised in the periodical *Prabasi* in 1929. It was published in book form later the same year. Krishna Kripalani's English translation, *Farewell, My Friend*, was published in London by the New India Publishing Company in 1946; an Indian edition of the translation (along with a translation of Tagore's novella *Malancha*) was published in Mumbai by Jaico Publishing House in 1956, as *Farewell, My Friend and The Garden*.

Shesher Kabita is Tagore's answer to his detractors within the Bengali literary establishment, particularly those associated with the *Kallol* group and others belonging to *Shanibarer Chithi* and *Kalikalam*. Tagore, at this time, was already troubled by the decline of his reputation in the west. In particular, he reacted against Edward Thompson's biography, *Rabindranath Tagore: Poet and Dramatist* (1921), and Katherine Mayo's *Mother India* (1927). Mayo had made unflattering allusions to Tagore's views on child marriage; Thompson, refuting the popular European perception of Tagore as a 'mystic' poet embodying the 'unbroken mind' of Bengal, had instead represented him as a poet who 'did not "have" an undisputed reputation; this reputation had still to be constructed (in India as in the west) by critical reappraisal, in the midst of a babel of conflicting opinions which stretched from detractors and envious competitors to uncritical "satellites".'[1]

On his home turf as well, Tagore had become a figure of controversy when he voiced his disenchantment with nationalism. Purists in the Bengali literary establishment had also attacked him for his use of 'chaltibhasha' or colloquial Bengali, rather than 'sadhubhasha' or chaste Bengali, in his writings. The burden of such criticism had made Tagore acutely insecure about his standing as a poet. According to Nirad C. Chaudhuri, 'He was abnormally sensitive, and did not possess the knack for cool disdain which a man of his social position naturally should have had'.[2] In a letter to Suniti Kumar Chattopadhyay dated 26 December 1929, Tagore complains: 'Generally speaking, we are naturally curious about someone who has been labelled controversial ... But the comments against me have been spiteful – to the effect that there is a multitude of flatterers who surround me and sing my praises and deprive me of the capacity to see my own failings'.[3] Nirad C. Chaudhuri argues, however, that this personal hostility would not have mattered so much but for a 'deeper and more radical opposition' between Tagore, who belonged to the liberal, monotheistic sect of the Brahmos, and other educated Bengalis of the Neo-Hindu conservative school. According to Chaudhuri, 'Tagore challenged all their political, social, cultural and religious superstitions, and was therefore regarded as an apostate. This gave to those who attacked him out of jealousy an appearance of respectability which otherwise they would not have had'.[4]

In literary terms, the debate between Tagore and his detractors centred upon the realism that was taken to be the yardstick of modernity. In 'The True Nature of Literature', Tagore declares: 'Too much tawdry poetising is now current in the name of *realism*. *Art* is not so cheap ... *realism* does not lie in the choice of theme: it must be brought out through the magic of writing'.[5] The critical controversies that surrounded Tagore found their forum for expression in a cluster of publications, including *Kallol*, *Shanibarer Chithi*, *Kalikalam*, *Bhabishyat*, *Pragati* and *Agragati*. The young writers of the Kallol group were especially vocal in their campaign for a new movement in literature. Challenging Tagore's iconic position in the literary establishment, they promoted Kazi Nazrul Islam and Saratchandra Chatterjee as their literary models. In 1927, Achintya Kumar Sengupta wrote in his poem 'Abishkar' ('Discovery'): 'Let my enemies fling at me countless sharp arrows, and let Rabindra Thakur sit in front of me obstructing my path, the sun of the age will pale in the intense flame I will light in my eyes. My way is longer'.[6] Nirad C. Chaudhuri attributes much of this animus to jealousy. He narrates an anecdote about the Bengali critic who, when asked to explain his grievance against Tagore, confessed: 'Shall I tell you the plain truth? We thought he and we were playmates in the same team, but suddenly discovered that he was very much above us. That, we could not tolerate.'[7] In 1928, Tagore organised a debate between his literary supporters and opponents in two sittings that took place at Bichitra Bhavan, Jorasanko. Representing the warring factions at the gathering, were Saratchandra Chatterjee, Nirad C. Chaudhuri, Achintya Kumar, Buddhadev Basu, Abanindranath Tagore, Suniti Kumar Chatterjee and other eminent litterateurs of the time. Tagore himself did not participate in the debate; he had already set out his views on literature and modernity in a cluster of recently published essays.

Sankha Ghosh argues that Tagore did not see the issues of the debate in black and white, because he was himself torn between the desire to preserve his former image and the urge to experiment with new styles of writing, commensurate with the demands of a changing intellectual climate.[8] *Farewell Song* is his attempt to negotiate this contradiction, a defence of his literary practice as well as a demonstration of his own credo of 'modernity' in literature. As Buddhadev Basu confesses, *Farewell Song*, when it first appeared, stunned Tagore's youthful literary opponents with its extraordinarily modern approach to writing:

> We felt as if a door that had not responded to the blows we had rained upon it with our inept hands had suddenly opened at a magician's touch. All that we had attempted without success, Rabindranath had accomplished – with such ease, so completely, and in such a beautiful way! It seemed the book was addressed to us, new writers, as an indirect admonition from Gurudev, intended to teach us a lesson. [9]

What these 'new writers' found most impressive was the brilliance of Tagore's language in the novel, for it had demonstrated the vitality and flexibility of the Bengali language, in ways they had not imagined possible. However, Basu also accuses Tagore of 'misusing' his own poetic genius in *Farewell Song*, for he finds an excess of lyricism in the novel. What emerges through these debates is an image of the complex love-hate relationship between Tagore, who was nearing seventy, and the younger writers of this period: a relationship that gave a fresh impetus to new schools of Bengali writing, even as it forced Tagore to reappraise his own oeuvre and dramatically alter his approach to fiction as he entered his final creative phase.

The passages of literary argument in the novel reveal Tagore's own capacity for intense self-scrutiny as he responded to the criticisms levelled against him. In *Kobir Shonge Dakshinatye*, Nirmal Kumari Mahalanobis describes how Tagore read aloud from his just-completed manuscript of *Farewell Song*, having stayed up all night to finish writing it.[10] In that version of June 1928, and in the two earliest manuscripts of the novel, transcribed by Amiya Chakravarty, there is no mention of the literary gathering of Tagore-lovers where Amit Raye makes his dramatic speech denouncing the old poet's decline and proclaiming the advent of a new poetic era. This speech was clearly added later; Sankha Ghosh sees it as a sign of Tagore's inability to shrug off the charges against his work. Although many of the verbal exchanges between Amit and Labanya are in verse, Ghosh argues that the literary debates in *Farewell Song* are not really essential to the love-plot. Amit and Labanya's arguments about poetry have less to do with their own developing romance than with Tagore's own fraught relationship with the young litterateurs of his time. Tagore emerges in Ghosh's account as a divided man, full of self-doubt, torn between the desire for public acceptance and the need to be true to his own literary ideals. From this internal upheaval arises the process of continual self-destruction and self-renewal that many readers regard as the defining feature of Tagore's work, especially during the final fifteen years of his life.

Some of this inner turmoil surfaces in Tagore's passion for painting during this phase of his creative life. Critics detect in the primitive energy of his drawings and paintings of this period an eruption of the repressed subconscious, an outpouring of all that he could not say in words. It is also remarkable that Tagore, at this time, wrote two novels very dissimilar in theme and treatment: *Yogayog* was serialised shortly before *Farewell Song*, and both novels appeared in book form in the same year. It was as if Tagore, in simultaneously engaging with two such different forms of fiction, was trying to channel the conflicting creative energies that were becoming increasingly hard to contain and harmonise.

Farewell Song also marks an important stage in Tagore's passion for experimenting with words, an obsession that had begun to manifest itself in *Ghare Baire* (*The Home and the World*), to culminate in the verbal intensity of *Char Adhyay* (*Four Chapters*). The language of *Farewell Song*, brilliantly epigrammatic, richly allusive and full of punning ambivalence, enacts the clash of literary ideologies that forms a vital strand of the narrative. Especially striking is the narrative voice, mocking, ironic, and at times scathingly satirical, but capable also of exquisite lyrical tenderness. For *Farewell Song* daringly breaches the dividing line between prose and poetry. Purists object to Tagore's dilution of the novel genre through his introduction of long passages of verse into the narrative, complaining that the work is neither fiction nor verse, but an impossible mixture of both. Yet, that, perhaps, is precisely Tagore's intention, as he reinvents the form of the Bengali novel to measure up to the contrary demands that he places upon it.

Dualities are in fact the defining feature of the novel's construction. Sankha Ghosh sees in Amit Raye an embodiment of this inner conflict, for Amit's apparent brashness masks his sensitivity to the ephemeral nature of literary fashion, a foreshadowing of the eventual triumph of Tagore's genius. Amit is aware that one day his own brand of 'modern' poetry will also become outdated, making way for a return to Tennyson and Byron. Two schools of Bengali poetry, pro- and anti-Tagore, are pitted against each other through the dialectic of the Amit-Labanya encounter. Two forms of love are presented through Amit's involvements with Katy Mitter and Labanya – one rooted in the earthly and the social, the other embedded deep within the soul. The sophisticated, artificial social world of Kolkata is contrasted with the idyllic natural environs of Shillong, an appropriate setting for the simple, yet dignified, existence of Labanya and Yogamaya. Though troubled by his own inner conflicts, Tagore also sees such tensions as productive. In a letter to Thomas Sturge Moore, he highlights the value of such a double vision, the capacity of literature to rejuvenate one's own culture by introducing 'foreign' elements, triggering self-division, a 'bifurcation' in the 'mental system which is so needful for all life growth'.[11]

The idea of a productive interaction of cultures also underlies the intertextuality that is such a distinctive feature of *Farewell Song*. The narrative is interspersed with allusions to Kalidasa, Bankim Chandra Chatterjee, Shakespeare, John Donne and Matthew Arnold, and to other major writers of England and India. Several of Tagore's own earlier works are alluded to as well. Lines from Vidyapati jostle with the brash poetry of Nibaran Chakrabarti. The allusions to English poetry, coupled with the depiction of the Anglicised upper-class society of

Kolkata, constitute Tagore's engagement with international-ism in this novel. While he was bitterly against the brutality of colonial rule, he felt that exposure to English education had enabled a new efflorescence of Bengali literature. 'English education is now inextricably fused with our society; we have thus acquired the right to judge freely what in it is good and what evil, what is major and what minor.'[12] According to Amartya Sen, Tagore opposed the oppressiveness of colonial rule, but welcomed the influence of English poetry as a source of enrichment for Bengali literature.[13] In a letter to Pramatha Chaudhuri (1891), Tagore writes:

> I sometimes detect in myself a battleground where two opposing forces are constantly in action, one beckoning me to peace and cessation of all strife, the other egging me on to do battle. It is as though the restless energy and the will to action of the West were perpetually assaulting the citadel of my Indian placidity. Hence this swing of the pendulum between passionate pain and calm detachment, between lyrical abandon and philosophising, between love of my country and mockery of patriotism, between an itch to enter the lists and a longing to remain wrapt in thought.[14]

Tagore's metaphor of the creative mind as a battleground for contending forces remains an apt description of his lifelong ambivalence about the 'East–West' encounter.

Central to the representation of this encounter in *Farewell Song* is the figure of Amit Raye, the novel's protagonist. Amit is believed by some to be modelled on Apurba Chanda, whose name finds mention in *The Oxonian*. It is a mistake, however, to entirely identify Amit with his companions, the members of Kolkata high society; for unlike them, he is capable of responding to Labanya's quiet, yet profound dignity. As the subject of the new Bengali novel, he is also given to self-scrutiny. From *Chokher Bali* (*Sand in the Eye*) (1903) onwards, Tagore self-consciously adopted what he considered to be the mode of the modern novel, eschewing external plot and action for a deeper focus on the inner psyche of his protagonists. Dipesh Chakrabarty notes this new quality of 'interiority' that marks the birth of the self-reflexive subject in the Bengali novel, the 'growing and close connection forged between literature, middle-class reading practices, and new forms of personhood' in Bengal during the early twentieth century.[15] Amit's pursuit of 'style' rather than 'fashion', and his adoption of the mask of Nibaran Chakrabarti, manifest the urge for self-fashioning that accompanied the emergence of the modern subject. This notion of identity as a construct challenges earlier ideas of an essential, immutable self. According to Chakrabarty, '[t]he collective subject whom we could call the Bengali-modern is perhaps better conceptualised as a mobile point on something like a relay network in which many different subject-positions and even non-bourgeois, non-individualistic practices of subjectivity intersected.'[16] The interiority of the modern Bengali subject adds a psychological dimension to the dichotomy between 'construction' and 'creation' as conceptualised by Tagore:

Construction is for a purpose, it expresses our wants; but … Creation is the revelation of truth through the rhythm of forms. It has a dualism consisting of the expression and the material. Of these two wedded companions the material must be kept in the background and continually offer itself as a sacrifice to its absolute loyalty to the expression. And this is true of all things, whether in our individual life or in our society.[17]

Clearly, 'form', for Tagore, is more than a literary issue: it underlies his very notions of self and society.

This is apparent in the debates about the true nature of modernity that form the subtext of *Farewell Song*. The allusive density of the novel derives, not from a desire to depict the clash of civilisations, but rather, to address the issues of tradition and modernity that caused such ferment in the Bengali literary scene at that time. 'It is evident that the modern age is riding on a tornado of rapidity', laments Tagore in 'The Philosophy of Leisure' (1929):

The perfection of our personality does not principally consist of qualities that generate cleverness or deftness or even accuracy of observation, or the rationality that analyses and forms generalisations. It depends mostly upon our training in truth and love, upon ideals that go to the root of our being.[18]

The arguments on poetry interwoven throughout the representation of the Amit-Labanya relationship serve to highlight the tensions between these two contrasting value-systems. Tagore's concern with style has as much to do with literary style, as with social modes. As Supriya Chaudhuri points out, 'there are styles of feeling, as of other aspects of civilised behaviour'.[19] According to her, this is related to 'new techniques of representation, whether in the usages of daily life or in the mimetic structures of literature and art'. *Farewell Song* is not only about different kinds of love, but also about different ways in which love may be represented. Labanya's views on love, for instance, are largely derived from books. 'The more I read the literature of love,' she tells Yogamaya, 'the more strongly I'm convinced that the tragedy of love occurs whenever people fail to accept their mutual independence, when they impose their will unjustly on others, when they imagine that we can change people, re-create them to suit our own desires.' Yogamaya draws attention to the new urge for refined analysis that has complicated the world-view of Labanya's generation. Literary representation and social self-fashioning are inextricably intertwined in Tagore's characterisation of Amit Raye/Nibaran Chakrabarti. In 'Modern Poetry' (1932) Tagore says: 'Today's modernity comes cut and dried, with short dress and cropped hair. Not that it never powders its cheeks or paints its lips, but it does so openly, with an insolent lack of inhibition.'[20] Though he is referring to changing trends in English poetry, this remark could well apply to the social image adopted by women of the Sissy-and-Lissy coterie in *Farewell Song*.

Farewell Song is the first novel by Tagore in which the action of the narrative is contemporaneous with the time of the novel's composition.[21] Literary satire combines with social satire in a scathing critique of fashionable conceptions of modernity current in Bengal during the late 1920s. Labanya's grandfather is a product of the social turbulence which the debate about English education had aroused a few decades earlier. The effects of an Oxford education are felt in the construction of Amit's person-alilty, although he writes poetry in Bengali and adopts a carefully indigenous style of dress. The characters in the novel present a spectrum of responses to the influence of European culture on Bengali society. At one end of the spectrum are Katy Mitter and her friends, members of the upper-class coterie culture of north Kolkata, who aped the external trappings of English high society in a blind pursuit of 'fashion'. At the opposite end are Yogamaya and Labanya, enriching their simple provincial existence with regular discussions on literary subjects, including English poetry. Straddling both worlds, but not quite belonging to either, Amit alternates between his fascina-tion for the superficial virtuosity of the Katy Mitter set and his deep attraction for the sober dignity of Labanya.

Similar tensions may be detected in the representation of gender relations in *Farewell Song*. Partha Chatterjee's argument about the stereotyping of woman as embodi-ment of 'purity' and repository of traditional value in nineteenth-century Bengal does not hold true for the elite society of Kolkata in the late 1920s, as depicted in *Farewell Song*.[22] Sissy, Lissy and Katy Mitter belong to a later generation of women, who are bent upon imitating the manners and lifestyle of the coloniser's culture. Even Labanya, 'untainted' though she is by such shallow urban fashions, cannot be taken to represent 'pure' Indian tradition, for she is an avid reader of English poetry, and defies social expectations by resisting marriage and leaving her parental home to become a governess. The text presents her as a signifier of positive value, invested with some of the qualities Tagore seeks to valorize as his answer to current definitions of modernity. She also serves as a yardstick by which the shallowness and artificiality of the Kolkata coterie culture is judged. All the same, Labanya, like Amit, remains a split subject, torn between her urge to safeguard her independence of spirit and her desire to surrender herself in love. Her eventual withdrawal from Amit seems almost inevitable, as if Tagore's imagination stopped short of visualising the actual triumph of Labanya's perspective if it were to be transplanted from Shillong into the urban social framework of Kolkata of which Amit is a part.

Specificities of time, place and history determine that Amit and Labanya must ultimately part company. In *Farewell Song*, societal pressures intrude upon the private world of romantic love, precluding its fulfillment in companionate marriage.[23] Amit's love for Labanya proves incompatible with the lifestyle and expectations of his own urban social milieu. A chastened and subdued Katy Mitter, who reverts to her earlier self as Ketaki, seems to him a more suitable partner for his everyday existence. But he continues to hunger for the ideal of romantic love, which resists containment within the boundaries of the mundane and the social. Labanya remains in Amit's heart as an image of this elusive ideal, while Ketaki becomes the spouse who will share with him the burdens of the workaday world.[24] He explains to Jatishankar: 'My relationship with Ketaki is indeed based on love, but it is like water in a pitcher, to be collected daily, and used up everyday. While my love for Labanya remains a lake, its waters not to be carried home, but meant for my consciousness to swim in.' The dualism thus remains unresolved, and Amit continues to be a split subject, committed simultaneously to two irreconcilable versions of love.

In its refusal to resort to facile reconciliations that would gloss over the literary, social and psychological turbulence that had riven Tagore's self and his world in the 1920s, *Farewell Song* stages the advent of the heterogeneous, unstable, modern Bengali subject. The text's engagement with literary and social controversies of the time anticipates many of the cultural and theoretical debates of today. Its self-conscious intertextuality contains within it the seeds of the comparatist approach that has acquired such prominence in present-day academia. Herein lies the clue, perhaps, to the novel's continued relevance. *Farewell Song* marks a crucial moment in the emergence of the modern novel; it alerts us to the need for a substantive reappraisal of Tagore and his place in world literature. The present translation is a step in that direction.

– Radha Chakravarty

Acknowledgements

I am grateful to Dr Rani Ray for her encouragement and advice, to Robin Harries for his careful scrutiny of the manuscript, to Isabel Wilkinson for the creative cover design and to my family for their patience and support.

Farewell Song

1
Speaking of Amit

Amit Rai is a barrister. Recast in the English mould, his surname, if transformed to 'Roy' or 'Ray', would lose its charm but gain many subscribers. Instead, seeking a touch of the unusual, Amit spelt his name so his English friends would pronounce it 'Amit Raye'.

Amit's father was a barrister of formidable repute. The fortune he had amassed was sufficient to ensure the moral downfall of the next three generations. But Amit managed to survive the terrible impact of his paternal legacy, emerging unscathed.

Before he was ready for graduate studies at Kolkata University, Amit entered Oxford. There, he spent seven years intermittently attempting his examinations, or abstaining from them. Because he was intelligent, he did not study very hard; yet it did not appear that he lacked learning. His father had no extraordinary expectations of him. He had only wanted his son to be so thoroughly steeped in the Oxford dye that it would not fade in the *desi* wash even after his return.

I like Amit. He's a fine fellow. I am a new writer with very few readers, of whom Amit is the worthiest. He is dazzled by the brilliance of my writing. He believes that in our literary marketplace, writers of repute have no style. Like the camel in the animal kingdom, their writings are ill-proportioned and awkward in gait, traversing only the bleak, barren desert of Bengali literature. Let me hasten to assure critics that this opinion is not mine.

Amit likens fashion to a mask, and style to beauty of countenance. Style, he feels, belongs to the literary elite, who live by their own wishes. And fashion is for the ordinary lot, who make it their business to please other people. The Bankim style may be seen in his own *Bishabriksha*; for in it, Bankim has found his *métier*. The Bankim fashion may be seen in Nasiram's *Manomohan's Mohanbagan*; for in it, Nasiram has reduced the original Bankim to dust. You may view a professional dancing girl beneath the awning of a public marquee; but for the first glimpse of the bride's face during the *shubhodrishti* ritual, a veil of Benarasi fabric is required. The marquee belongs to fashion, the Benarasi veil – which reveals the special one's countenance shaded by a special hue – to style. Amit says it's because we're afraid to venture beyond the beaten track that style is held in such low esteem in our country. A scriptural elaboration of this idea may be found in the Dakshayajna story in the Puranas. Indra, Chandra and Varun, the fashionable deities in the celestial world, would be invited to events in the *yajna* circuit. But Shiva had style; he was so original that the prayer-chanting priests who performed these sacrificial ceremonies thought it improper to offer him oblations. I like hearing such words from someone with a B.A. degree from Oxford. For I believe my writing has style. That is why all my books attain *moksha* in single editions, liberated from the cycle of rebirth, never to appear again.

My wife's brother, my *shala* Nabakrishna, couldn't stand Amit's talk. 'To hell with his Oxford degree!' he'd protest. A prodigiously impressive M.A. in English literature, he had studied a lot, and understood little.

'Amit always lionises minor writers, only to belittle major ones,' he observed to me the other day. 'It suits his fancy to drum up a show of contempt, and you serve as his drumstick.'

Sad to say, my wife, his very own sister, was present at this discussion. But it's supremely gratifying to note that she didn't like my *shala*'s words at all. Her taste matched Amit's, I observed, although she wasn't highly educated. How amazing is the natural intelligence of women!

Sometimes, I, too, have some doubts, seeing that Amit has no compunctions even about denigrating many well-known English writers. These are writers of the mass market, branded with the label of greatness. You need not read these writers in order to admire them, for in order to pass your examinations you need only sing their praises blindly. Amit, too, does not need to read their works, for he has no hesitation in criticising them blindly. Actually, he finds the most famous writers too publicly official, like the waiting room at Burdhwan station; while the authors he has himself discovered are his own exclusive territory, like the saloon compartment of a special train.

Style is Amit's passion. Not just in his literary taste, but also in his dress and manners. His very appearance is cast in a special mould. He is not a common person, but one who stands out among many. You'd notice him in a crowd. A rounded countenance, clean-shaven and gleaming, with a dark, glowing complexion; a lively manner, restless eyes, restless smile, restless gait and gestures, quick at repartee; his mind a flint that emits sparks if tapped ever so slightly. He often wears homespun fabric, because members of his social set don't. He sports a *dhoti* of white cotton yardage, carefully pleated, because this style is not fashionable among his peers. The buttons on his *kurta* run diagonally from the left shoulder down to the right side of his midriff. The sleeve is slit right to the elbow. On his left hip, from a broad brown *zari*-trimmed waistband, hangs a small printed pouch containing his pocket-watch. His feet are shod in Cuttack-style white leather shoes with red leather trimming. When he ventures out, a folded Madras scarf, embellished with a border, is draped over his left shoulder, down to his knees. When invited to friends' homes, he wears a Muslim-style Lucknow cap, embroidered white on white. I wouldn't quite describe this as dressing up: it's more like a loud burst of laughter. I don't comprehend his western garb, but those in the know tell me it's somewhat dishevelled, yet *distinguished*, as they say in English. He feels no urge to beautify himself, but has boundless relish for mocking fashion. Those who claim to be young by virtue of their age and birth-chart are a dime a dozen; but Amit's rare youthfulness is the result of his pure immaturity, utterly heedless, flighty, like a flood-tide carrying all in its wake as it rushes forth, holding nothing back.

Meanwhile, his two sisters, nicknamed Sissy and Lissy, are like the latest merchandise in the market, carefully packaged from head to toe according to the reigning vogue. High-heeled shoes, low-cut lace-trimmed jacket revealing necklaces of coral and amber, sari draped aslant, wrapped tightly around the body. They walk with a tripping gait, speak in loud voices, and modulate their peals of shrill laughter. Head tilted slightly, they glance obliquely upwards with a faint smile; they know the art of a meaningful look. Every now and then, they flutter a pink silk fan close to their cheeks, and perched on the arm of their menfriends' chairs, they rap their admirers with the fan in feigned protest against the men's feigned impertinence.

Within his social circle, Amit's male friends are envious of his way with women. Amit is not particularly indifferent to women, nor does he seem particularly attracted by anyone; yet, he never lacks romantic charm. In a word, what he feels for women is not passion but enthusiasm. Amit attends parties, plays card-games, loses wagers on purpose, urges tone-deaf women to sing and if someone wears an unsuitable colour, enquires where such fabric may be bought. He adopts a tone of special partiality when addressing any female acquaintance; yet everyone knows that his show of favouritism masks total indifference. He who worships many gods secretly hails each deity as superior to the others; though perfectly aware of this, the gods can't help feeling flattered all the same. The mothers of marriageable daughters refuse to give up hope, but the brides-to-be realise that Amit is a golden, ever-receding horizon, always available, yet never to be captured. About women, his mind is in perpetual debate, never reaching a conclusion. This explains his daring in plunging into intimacies that are blind alleys, leading nowhere. That is why he gets along with everyone so easily; for even in the presence of inflammatory substances, he is safely insulated from catching fire.

Once, at a riverside picnic, when the moon rose above the deep, dark, intense silence on the opposite shore of the Ganges, Lily Ganguly was by his side.

'The new moon across the river, and you and me together, on this shore,' he murmured to her in a low voice. 'Such a conjugation will never occur again in all eternity.'

For an instant, Lily Ganguly's heart had lurched with brimming emotion; but she knew these words only as true as the style of their utterance. To claim anything more would be like reaching for the rainbow above the bubbles. So, jerking herself out of her momentary trance, Lily laughed: 'Amit, what you say is so obviously true that you need not have said it at all. Even that frog leaping into the water is an event never to recur in all eternity.'

'There's a difference, Lily,' smiled Amit, 'a vast difference. Tonight, the leap of that frog is a disjointed, fragmented event. But taken together, you and I, the flow of the Ganges, and the stars in the sky, have created a complete harmony – like Beethoven's Moonlight Sonata. I think there's an insane goldsmith in the celestial workshop of Viswakarma, maker of the world. Having carved these three hours into a perfect golden ring set with sapphires, diamonds and emeralds, he has instantly cast it into the ocean, never to be found again.'

'All the better, Amit, for now you need not worry about settling accounts with Viswakarma's goldsmith.'

'But Lily, after a million ages, beside some thousand-mile long canal, in the red forest-shadows of Mars, should you and I perchance come face to face, and if that fisherman in the Shakuntala story should slit the catfish's belly to retrieve for us this exquisite golden moment, we would gaze at each other, startled. But imagine what would happen thereafter.'

'Thereafter, the golden moment would sink unnoticed into the sea,' retorted Lily, rapping Amit with her fan. 'Never to be found again. We've lost count of all those other moments, crafted by the insane goldsmith and discarded by you, because you have forgotten them.'

With these words, Lily hastened away to join her female friends. This episode is an example of many other such events in Amit's life.

'Ami, why don't you get married?' Amit's sisters Sissy-and-Lissy asked him, once.

'For marriage, a *paatri* – a prospective bride – is the first requirement,' replied Amit, 'and after that, the *paatra* – the prospective groom.'

'You surprise me,' exclaimed Sissy. 'There are so many women!'

'Women were sought in marriage in olden times, when horoscopes were matched,' declared Amit. 'I want a *paatri* worthy of the role, whose own self is her identity, second to none.'

'Once she enters your home, you will take precedence, and she will occupy second place,' Sissy pointed out. 'Her identity will be defined by yours.'

'The woman I secretly await in vain as the right match for me has no fixed address,' replied Amit. 'She usually doesn't make it to my threshold. A falling star, she bursts into flames as soon as she enters my heart's atmosphere and vanishes into thin air, without ever reaching my earthly abode.'

'Meaning, she's a far cry from your sisters,' retorted Sissy.

'Meaning, if she were to join our household, she would be more than an addition to the family,' answered Amit.

'Tell me, dear Sissy,' interrupted Lissy, 'why doesn't Ami fancy Bimi Bose, who waits so eagerly, and would come running at the slightest signal from him? She lacks culture, he says. Why, my dear, she stood first in M.A. Botany! Education is culture, after all.'

'The stone of the kamal-diamond is education, and the light that radiates from it is culture,' explained Amit. 'The stone has weight, and the light, brilliance.'

'Oh, he has no time for Bimi Bose!' cried Lissy, enraged. 'If ever Ami has a mad desire to marry her, I'll warn Bimi Bose not to spare him a second glance.'

'Why would I want to marry Bimi Bose unless I was indeed mad?' demanded Amit. 'If that ever happens, please consider medical treatment, rather than marriage, for me.'

Their relatives had given up hoping that Amit would ever marry. They had concluded that, being unfit for the responsibilities of married life, he dreamt of the impossible and went about trying to impress people with his perverse talk. His heart was a will-o'-the-wisp, dazzling if seen outdoors, but impossible to capture and bring home.

Meanwhile, Amit socialised with abandon, treating stray acquaintances to tea at Firpo's, taking friends on unnecessary motor-car drives whenever the fancy took him, buying odd items from here and there and giving them away to all and sundry, leaving newly purchased English books in friends' homes and forgetting to retrieve them.

His sisters were particularly annoyed by his habit of airing contrary views. He was always sure to contradict the ideas approved by civilised society.

Once, when some political theorist waxed eloquent about the virtues of democracy; Amit exclaimed: 'When Vishnu dismembered Sati's body, more than a hundred scattered places of pilgrimage sprang up across the country. Today, democracy has produced a host of sites for the worship of small, fragmented aristocracies. The world has been taken over by minor aristocrats – in politics, literature, and society. They lack seriousness, all of them, for they have no faith in themselves.'

On another occasion, a philanthropist, championing the cause of helpless women, blamed men for the oppression of women under patriarchy. Suddenly, Amit removed the cigarette from his lips and blurted out: 'If men surrender their authority, women will at once begin to dominate. The dominance of the weak is a fearsome thing.'

'What's that supposed to mean?' angrily demanded the helpless women and all their champions present at the gathering.

'One with shackles at his disposal would tame the bird with them,' replied Amit. 'In other words, he would use force. One who owns no shackles must subdue the bird with opium – in other words, with charm. The user of shackles can exercise control, but no charm; the user of opium can exercise control as well as charm. A woman's pill-box is full of opium, and wicked Nature keeps up the supply.'

One day, at a literary gathering in Baliganj, the poetry of Rabindranath Tagore was the subject of discussion. For the first time in his life, Amit had agreed to preside over the discussion. He had arrived mentally armed for battle.

The speaker was a very simple, old-fashioned man. His aim was to prove that Robi Thakur's verse was indeed real poetry. Barring a couple of college professors, most members of the audience acknowledged that the proof he offered was more or less satisfactory.

'Every poet should enjoy a five-year term for writing verse, from the age of twenty-five to thirty,' declared the chairperson, rising to his feet. 'What we expect from the next generation is not something better, but something different. When the season for Fazli mangoes is over, we wouldn't clamour for a better variety of the same fruit. We'd say, 'Fetch us some good-sized custard-apples from New Market, sir.' A green coconut has a brief shelf-life, as long as it has juice; a ripe coconut lasts much longer, for it's the substance that counts. Poets are short-lived, but philosophers outlive trees and stones... The greatest complaint against Robi Thakur is that, in imitation of old man Wordsworth, this gentleman has lived unfairly long. Yama, god of death, repeatedly sends his henchmen to extinguish his life, but the man still stands, clutching the arm of his chair for support. If he doesn't voluntarily make a dignified exit, it would be our collective duty to withdraw from his literary circle. His successor, too, will declaim, in rhythmic metre, that the sun doesn't set on his empire, for he holds the celestial city Amaravati chained to his threshold, here on earth. For a while, devotees will offer him garlands and sandalwood paste, keep him well-fed, prostrate themselves at his feet. Then will come the holy date for his ritual slaughter, the auspicious moment of his devotees' release from their bondage to him. In Africa, four-footed deities are worshipped in the same way. The worship of two-footed, three-footed, four-footed and fourteen-footed gods of verse also follows the same rule. There can be nothing more impure and corrupt than to render the ritual of worship monotonous… Taste is subject to evolution. If taste remains static where it was five years ago, it becomes painfully evident that it's unaware of its own demise. At the slightest nudge, the deceased must confront the fact that his sentimental kinfolk have postponed his last rites, perhaps to permanently delude his worthy successors. I have vowed to publicly expose this illicit conspiracy of the Robi Thakur faction.'

'Do you want to remove loyalty from the world of literature?' asked our friend Manibhushan, his spectacles flashing.

'Absolutely. Here begins the age of the short-lived poet-president. The second thing I want to say about Robi Thakur is that his literary works are like his handwriting: rounded or undulating, like a rose or a woman's face, or the moon. This is primitive, an imitation of Nature's script. From the new President, we require lines that are sharp and straight – like arrows, like spearheads, like thorns. Not like flowers, but like streaks of lightning. Like the pain of neuralgia. Cast in the mould of a Gothic church with sharp angles and corners, not like the *mandap* or prayer-pavilion in a temple. No harm, indeed, if its shape resembles a jute-mill or a secretariat building… From now on, discard the artistry of rhyme and metre designed to charm the reader's heart; we must seize the reader's heart by force, as Ravana had abducted Sita. The heart may weep and protest when dragged away, but go along it must. Jatayu, that ancient creature, will appear on the scene to remonstrate, and lose his life in the process. Soon after, Kiskindhya will be stirred to action, and suddenly, some Hanuman will leap into Lanka, setting it ablaze, in order to rescue the heart and bring it back home. A reunion with Tennyson will follow; we'll cling to Byron, weeping profusely; we'll beg Dickens' forgiveness for having cursed him in our urge to cure ourselves of enchantment... If all the enchanted workmen of India, from Mughal times to the present day, were to build domed marble bubbles across the country, then every *bhadralok* or gentleman would hasten to renounce the world the day he crossed twenty, to live like a hermit in the woods. We must destroy the magic of the Taj Mahal precisely in order to restore the Taj Mahal's attraction.'

(At this juncture, it must be added that, unable to cope with the flood of words, the rapporteur at the gathering had grown dizzy. His report proved even more unintelligible than Amit's lecture. We have presented above the few fragments of it that we could retrieve.)

At the mention of the revival of interest in the Taj Mahal, a devotee of Robi Thakur exclaimed, 'We can never have too much of a good thing.'

'Quite the contrary,' declared Amit. 'In this world, good things are valued because they are rare, or else overabundance would render them mediocre... Poets who are not ashamed of surviving to be sixty or seventy invite punishment by cheapening themselves. Ultimately, they find themselves trapped, hemmed in by the mimicry of their band of imitators. Their writing becomes warped; beginning to steal from their own earlier works, they become

14

receivers of stolen goods. In such situations, for the general public good, it is the duty of readers to ensure at all costs that such overage poets are not allowed to survive; I speak of survival in the poetic, not the physical sense. Let their longevity be transferred instead to elderly professors, politicians and critics.'

'Who would you like for president, may I know?' demanded the speaker of the day. 'Please name the candidate.'

'Nibaran Chakrabarti,' replied Amit, in a flash.

There was a murmur of surprise from different segments of the audience: 'Nibaran Chakrabarti? Who's that?'

'Today's question is a mere seedling, the answer to which will rear its head tomorrow, like a giant tree.'

'Meanwhile, we'd like a sample of his work.'

'Listen, then.' He produced a long, slim, canvas-bound notebook from his pocket and began to read aloud from it:

> *'I herald the advent*
> *Of the Unknown One, announcing*
> *His name to the world,*
> *To known faces in public streets.*
> *A newcomer, I deride*
> *The ways of the ordinary rabble.*
> *Open your doors!*
> *For I bear heaven's message,*
> *In script inscrutable,*
> *Inscribed by Time.*
> *Say, who dares reply,*
> *Who dares to stake his life*
> *On the difficult answer?*

They will not listen;
Folly's army
Blocks my path.
Cry of fruitless anger,
Crashing upon my breast,
Like the futile waves
That beat their heads in vain
Against the rocky shore,
In self-destructive pride.

'I wear no flower-garlands; no armour
Shields the bareness of my breast.
On my forehead's empty page is drawn
A deep mark of victory,
A tattered wrap my poor man's garb.
I'll deplete your treasure-house.
Open, open your doors!
Suddenly,
I extend my hand:
Delay not, give me what you will.
Your heart flutters, the door-latch trembles,
Your world is in turmoil,

'The horizon rent
With fearful screams:
'Away at once,
Unquiet beggar!
Time and time again
Your voice assails
Our deep nocturnal slumber.'

'Where are your weapons?
Rattle your sabres, stab me in the side!
      Let death destroy death; let my immortal life
            Be my legacy.
      Enchain me, then!
Tie me down! At once, I'll break my bonds,
      And claiming liberty, set you free.

      'Where are your scriptures?
Attack me with them.
      In learned dispute
Let's loudly defy
            The divine decree.
      I know for sure, the arrows of debate
Will be shattered. Our eyes,
      With worn words long befogged,
            Shall see the light again.

            'Ignite the fire!
If what's good today
      Should tomorrow be charred,
      Burnt to ashes
      Worldwide,
      So let it be.
Feel no sorrow.
Let my ordeal by fire
Bring glory to the world.

      'My obscure words
Will deal a stunning blow,
      To subdue the obdurate

With shock and fear.
My wild rhymes
Will alike perplex
Seekers after salvation,
And creatures of appetite.
They'll beat their brows, and one by one,
In anger, pain or fear,
They'll accept the public victory
Of the Unknown One.
The Unknown One!
Who rocks the world
With fiery Baisakh storms;
Smashes the cloud-banks with a mighty blow
To unleash their hidden hoard of rain.
And tears the world apart, to set it free.'

On that occasion, Robi Thakur's supporters were silenced. They departed, threatening to respond in writing.

'You must have created Nibaran Chakrabarti in advance, and carried him in your pocket, just to fool all the simpletons,' observed Sissy to Amit as he drove home, after having dumbfounded his audience.

'He who promotes someone yet to arrive, is known as god of the unarrived,' replied Amit. 'That's what I am. Today, Nibaran Chakrabarti has arrived in this world; there's no stopping him now.'

Sissy was secretly very proud of Amit. 'Tell me, Amit,' she asked, 'Do you prepare all your well-honed speeches, just like the latest one, as soon as you get up in the morning?'

'It is the essence of civilisation to be ready for all eventualities,' declared Amit. 'Barbarity is unprepared for everything in this world. This thought is also recorded in my notebook.'

'But you have no opinion of your own, blurting out whatever sounds good in a particular situation.'

'My mind is a mirror. If I were to leave it forever smeared with my own fixed views, it would cease to reflect the image of every passing moment.'

'Ami, you will spend your life chasing images in a mirror,' warned Sissy.

2
Encounter

Amit chose to visit the hills of Shillong, because members of his social circle didn't frequent the place and also because the flood of marriage proposals would be less overwhelming there. The deity with the love-bow who constantly hovered over Amit's heart preferred to haunt only fashionable areas. Of all the hill-resorts in the region, Shillong offered him the most restricted scope for target-practice.

Amit's sisters shook their heads. 'Go alone if you must,' they said. 'We're not coming with you.'

Carrying folding parasols of the latest style in their left hand and tennis racquets in their right, cloaked in fake-Parisian shawls, off went the sisters to Darjeeling. Bimi Bose had already reached the place. When the sisters arrived minus their brother, she cast her eyes about and discovered that Darjeeling had people, but no real men.

Amit had informed everyone in parting that he was going to Shillong to savour the solitude. Within a couple of days, he realised that in the absence of people, solitude lost its flavour. Amit had no taste for roaming with a camera in search of scenic beauty. I'm not a tourist, he'd say; I like to taste things with my mind, not swallow them with my eyes.

He spent a few days reading in the shade of deodar trees on the hill-slopes. He didn't touch fiction, for reading fiction while on holiday smacked of ordinariness. He began to read Suniti Chatterjee's philology of the Bengali language, hoping intensely that he would disagree with the author. From time to time, at intervals between his study of grammar and his spells of indolence, the hills and forests of this place would suddenly strike him as beautiful, but it stirred no intense emotion in his heart. It was like a monotonous *alaap*, the prelude to a performance of classical music, with no refrain, no *taal* or rhythm, and no *sam* to emphasise the recurring main beat in a rhythmic cycle. In other words, his outlook was wide-ranging but lacked focus; to his eyes, everything seemed diffuse and scattered, failing to coalesce. In the universe of his own self, this lack of internal coherence caused Amit constantly and restlessly to disperse his identity. He found this as distressing in Shillong as in the city. But in an urban setting, he managed to expend this restlessness in many ways; here, it persisted, and accumulated, like the pool that forms when a waterfall's path is obstructed. He had begun to contemplate escaping downhill on foot, wandering at will through Shillong and Shilchar. Just then the Ashadh rains descended, across the hills and through the woods, spreading their shadowy cloak of moisture-laden clouds. News arrived that the mountain-peaks of Cherrapunji had faced the onslaught of the gathering early monsoon clouds. Now, heavy showers would incite the mountain waterfalls to madness, urging them to break their bounds. He decided that the occasion demanded a visit to the dak-bungalow of Cherrapunji, where the spirit of *Meghdoot* must be invoked. There, his powerful rendering of the Cloud-Messenger's invisible thunder would impel the heroine to streak across his mental skyline like disembodied lightning, leaving behind neither her signature, nor any address.

On that day, he donned thick highland socks, sturdy, thick-soled leather boots, a khaki Norfolk tunic, knee-length shorts, and on his head, a *sola* hat. He didn't quite resemble a Yaksha in an Abani Thakur illustration, but he could have been taken for a district engineer out to inspect the roads. In his pocket, though, were three or four slim volumes of poetry in different languages.

The path was narrow and tortuous, a forest-covered precipice on his right. This was the way to Amit's lodgings. There was no likelihood of encountering traffic here, so he drove rashly, without sounding the horn. At that very moment, he was thinking that the motor car, in modern times, is the appropriate messenger for a distant beloved; for it combines elements of smoke and fire, desert and sea, in the right proportions, and a letter sent through the driver can get one's message across, in no uncertain terms. In the coming year, he decided, at the very onset of the Ashadh rains, he would drive down the path described in *Meghdoot*. For perhaps fate would spare him a kind glance to ensure that the beloved – Avantika or Malavika, or some wanderer in the deodar forests – would appear before him, to fulfill some unthinkable destiny. At this moment, he suddenly arrived at a bend in the road to see another car making its way upwards. There was no space for the vehicles to pass each other. Stepping on the brakes, he drove right up to the car; they collided, but there was no mishap. The other car rolled a little way down to stop at the edge of the hillside.

A young woman alighted from the vehicle. Against the dark backdrop of their narrow escape from death, she stood out like a clear picture drawn in streaks of lightning, independent of everything around her. Like Lakshmi arising from the foaming sea when it was churned by the Mandar mountain, the woman was above all the turmoil, although the waves of the great ocean continued to heave and swell. Amit took this rare opportunity to observe her. In a drawing room, in company, he would not have perceived this woman in all her uniqueness. In this world, one may sometimes find a person worth gazing at; but a suitable location for the viewing is rarely to be found.

The woman was dressed in a white, narrow-bordered sari, a jacket made of the same warm fabric, and white shoes of a *desi* pattern. She was tall, with a dark, glowing complexion; her large eyes, shaded by heavy eyelashes, had a tender intensity; her hair was tied back, swept away from her broad forehead; her beautifully rounded face and chin had the charm of an unripe fruit. The sleeves of her jacket came up to her elbows; on her wrists, she wore a pair of slim, plain bangles. The end of her sari, not confined by a brooch at her shoulder, was draped over her head, held in place with a silver filigree hairpin.

Leaving his hat in the car, Amit came and stood silently before her, as if awaiting some punishment that was his due. At this, the young woman showed some signs of pity, mingled with amusement.

'I am at fault,' apologised Amit, in a low voice.

'No fault, but an error,' smiled the woman. 'The error began with me.'

Her voice was pure, like the water bubbling forth from a spring. Smooth and full, like the voice of a young boy. When he returned home that day, Amit spent a long time trying to conjure up words to describe the music of this voice, its taste and texture. Opening his notebook, he wrote: 'It's like the light, hazy smoke of ambergris-scented tobacco as it spirals through water, not with the pungency of nicotine, but with the tender fragrance of rose water.'

'I had gone out in search of a friend after receiving news of her arrival,' said the woman, to explain her error. 'As soon as we'd climbed a little way up this road, the chauffeur pointed out that we were on the wrong route. By then it was too late to turn back without driving all the way to the top. That's why we were on our way up, when higher powers assaulted us.'

'There is a power beyond the higher powers – a hideous, evil planet, whose adverse influence has brought this about.'

'There's not much damage done,' the driver of the other vehicle informed them, 'but it will take a while to fix the car.'

'If you forgive my car for the offence just committed, I could drive you wherever you permit,' offered Amit.

'There's no need, I'm used to walking in the hills.'

'The need is mine, as proof that I am forgiven.'

The woman remained silent, seeming a little hesitant.

'I have something more to say,' declared Amit. 'I drive fast – not a worthy thing to do, for I can't drive this vehicle into the realm of posterity. Yet, that is your first and only impression of me. But even that is caught in a snag, worse luck. As an epilogue to this drama, please let me demonstrate that, in this realm, at least, I am not inferior to your chauffeur.'

When they first meet a stranger, women are reluctant to relinquish their reserve, fearing unknown dangers. But the trauma of imminent danger had broken down her fences in a single blow, rendering preliminaries unnecessary. Some unknown divinity, lacking patience, had brought the two of them face to face on a solitary mountain road, and fused their hearts together. The lightning-flash of this sudden revelation would haunt them often at night, etching itself against the darkness. Like the flaming imprint of sun and stars on the azure of the sky during some great cosmic collision, it left a deep impression within their consciousness.

Without a word, she entered his car. Following her directions, they arrived at her destination.

'Please drop in tomorrow, if you have the time,' she suggested, stepping out of the car. 'I'll introduce you to the lady of the house.'

'I have all the time in the world; I could drop in right away,' Amit felt like blurting out. But he was too embarrassed to utter the words.

Back home, he wrote in his notebook: 'What madness awaited us on the road I took today! It wrenched the two of us from our different moorings, and set us on the same track, perhaps. The astronomer was wrong. From some unknown galaxy, the moon had descended into the earth's orbit. Like vehicles, they collided, and ever since that near-death experience, they move together through the ages, the two of them, their radiance illuminating each other's countenance. Their mutual bond keeps them together as they travel. My heart tells me, here begins our journey together. As we travel, we shall string together, moment by moment, a garland of the bright instants garnered along our way. We can no longer depend upon fate, hoping for a safe, predictable life, with a fixed salary and a fixed livelihood; all our exchanges will be sudden and unexpected.'

Outside, it was raining. 'Nibaran Chakrabarti, where are you?' exclaimed Amit to himself, as he paced the verandah. 'Come, possess me now. Give me words, give me words.' Out came the long, slim notebook, and Nibaran Chakrabarti declaimed:

'We travel on the drifting breeze, bound
By our journey's invisible ties.
　　　In our hearts, a festival of colour, wrought
By this bright-hued moment, darling of the dust,
　　　The horizon dances, flashing
　　　　　Its veil across the rainclouds.
Its sudden radiance
　　　Dazzles the mind.

'Not for us the kanak-champa groves,
Nor forest-arbours full of bakul clusters.
　　　At dusk, some unknown flower
　　　Spreads its sudden fragrance
　　　　　At dawn, as if mocking
　　　The rosy clouds,
On the treetops bloom
　　　Bunches of rhododendron.

'Not for us the wealth of hoarded treasure,
Not for us the love and care of home.
　　　We seek not to encage
The bird that flutters past,
　　　Content to hear the song

27

Of that winged freedom-lover.
Irradiated are we, by the rare glory
Of the unimaginable.'

At this point, we must pause for retrospection. Once we have disposed of the past, our narrative can proceed unhindered.

3
A backward glance

During the first phase of English education in Bengal, a storm had erupted over the disparity between *chandimandaps* for the worship of Durga, and educational institutions like schools and colleges. Gyanadashankar had surrendered to the turbulence of that social revolution. He belonged to the older generation, but had been suddenly catapulted into the modern age. He was born ahead of his time. In intelligence, speech and behaviour, he was unlike his contemporaries. Like a bird that loves to ride the sea-waves, he took pleasure in baring his breast to onslaughts of public blame.

When the grandchildren of such forefathers try to make amends for such reversals of date and time, they rush to the opposite extreme, the terminus at the other end of the almanac. So it was in this case, as well. After his father's demise, Gyandashankar's grandson Baradashankar regressed almost to the era of his grandfather's early ancestors. He would worship Manasa, goddess of snakes, and simultaneously try to appease Sheetala, the deity of smallpox, by addressing her as 'Ma'. He began to drink water in which amulets had been rinsed, and spent entire mornings inscribing the thousand names of Durga. The Vaishyas in his locality, who were out to prove their scriptural erudition, were harassed in public and in private. To preserve the customs intended to protect Hinduism from the corrupting touch of science, he lavishly showered free words of wisdom upon the modern mind, through countless pamphlets printed with the assistance of the Bhat community, people of mixed caste. In a very short time, through holy rituals, meditation and penance, baths, incense, and devoted service of cows and Brahmins, he ensured that his immovable fortress of religious purity became completely impregnable. At twenty-seven, he ultimately left for his heavenly abode, carrying with him the blessings of countless Brahmins in exchange for having donated cows, gold and land, in the name of his father, mother and daughters.

Barada had been married to Yogamaya, daughter of Ramlochan Bannerji, his father's close friend, college-mate and companion from the days when they frequented restaurants for chops-and-cutlets. At that particular time, there was no class-difference in the lifestyles of Yogamaya's parental and marital homes. The women in her family were educated. They appeared in society, and some had even published travelogues in illustrated monthly magazines. Coming from such a family, she found herself married to a man who strove to prevent the slightest lapse in her adherence to the rituals of purity. Yogamaya's movements were restricted by various passport procedures designed to safeguard the boundaries of religious orthodoxy, fixed by unshakable moral law. A veil descended over her eyes, and over her mind. If Saraswati, goddess of learning, ever found the time to pay them a visit, even she had to undergo a security check before being allowed into the private quarters of their house. The English books she carried were confiscated at the outer gate itself; if detected, Bengali writings published after the pre-Bankim era could not cross the inner threshold. For a long time, a beautifully bound edition of the

Yogabashishtha Ramayana in Bengali translation lay on Yogamaya's shelf, awaiting her attention. That she would one day take it up by way of pastime, was a wish the master of the house had cherished to his dying day. It was not easy for Yogamaya to fold herself into the iron safe of antiquity like a deposit, but she had reined in her rebellious mind. In this mental prison, her only refuge was Deenasharan Vedantaratna, the family priest. He appreciated Yogamaya's clear, natural intelligence.

'Ma, all these wasteful religious rituals are not for you,' he would succinctly declare. 'The foolish not only delude themselves, but are deceived by everything under the sun. Do you think we believe in any of these things? Don't you see how it pains me to distort the scriptures by twisting the syntax as occasion demands? In other words, we reject these restrictions in private, but must outwardly pretend to be fools, to please those who are foolish. If you are unwilling to be deluded, I cannot undertake to deceive you. Please send for me whenever you wish, Ma; I shall read to you from the scriptures only what I believe to be true.'

Sometimes, he would visit Yogamaya and explicate passages from the *Gita* or the *Brahmabhashya*. Vedantaratna was delighted at Yogamaya's intelligent questions and had boundless enthusiasm for discussions with her. For the hangers-on – important or otherwise – who surrounded Baradashankar, Vedantaratna had immense contempt.

'Ma, yours is the only house in this entire city, where I find pleasure in conversation,' he would assure Yogamaya. 'You have saved me from self-contempt.'

In this way, amidst a relentless routine of rituals and fasts, days passed by, chained to the dictates of the holy almanac. Her whole life became a matter of 'fulfilling her obligations', as they say in the bizarre language of today's newspapers. Immediately after her husband's demise, she took to traveling, accompanied by her son Jatishankar and daughter Suroma. She would spend the winter in Kolkata, and the summer in some mountain resort. Jatishankar was now a college-student; but unable to locate a girls' school suitable for Suroma's education, she managed to find, after much searching, a teacher called Labanyalata. This was the woman Amit had suddenly encountered, early that morning.

4
All about Labanya

Labanya's father Abanish Dutta was principal of a college in the western region. He had brought up his motherless daughter in such a way that even the struggle to pass numerous examinations had not diminished her intellectual powers. In fact, she still retained an intense love of learning.

Learning, the father's only passion, had found complete vicarious fulfillment through his daughter. She was dearer to him than his own library. He believed that a mind honed in the pursuit of learning was like an impermeable slab of concrete through which the gases of frivolous emotions could never penetrate from below. Hence, a person with such a mind had no need for marriage. He was firmly convinced that the portion of his daughter's heart which could have provided tender, fertile soil for marriage and motherhood had been hardened to cement by mathematics and history – a heart extremely strong and firm, scratch-resistant, immune to external assaults. He had even imagined that, if Labanya did not marry, she could remain forever wedded to learning.

There was someone else he doted on. The young man's name was Shobhanlal. One rarely encountered such a deep interest in studies from such an early age. With his broad forehead, clear gaze, pleasant set of the lips, simple smile, and handsome countenance, his appearance was instantly attractive to the viewer's eye. He was extremely self-effacing, flustered if anyone paid him the slightest attention.

He was a poor man's son. Step by step, aided by scholarships, he cleared the insurmountable peaks of numerous examinations. His professor anticipated with pride that Shobhan would one day be famous, and that Abanish's own name would head the list of those who had chiefly engineered this success. Shobhan came to his house to receive instruction; he had free access to the library. He would cringe in embarrassment if he saw Labanya. This embarrassment created a distance between them, leaving Labanya free to imagine herself his superior. Women don't notice a hesitant man who does not assertively draw attention to himself.

Meanwhile, Shobhanlal's father Nonigopal arrived one day at Abanish's residence and cursed him roundly. He complained that, on the pretext of offering tuition at home, Abanish hoped to trap the boy into marriage with his daughter, to satisfy his urge for social reform by ruining the caste-purity of Shobhanlal, a Vaidya's son. As proof of his accusations, he submitted a pencil-sketch of Labanyalata. The drawing, covered in rose-petals, had been discovered inside Shobhanlal's tin trunk. Nonigopal had no doubt that the picture was a love-token gifted by Labanya herself. In his calculating mind, Nonigopal had worked out, to the last detail, Shobhanlal's current value in the marriage market, and how much it was likely to increase if one waited patiently for a short while. Abanish's ploy for seizing this valuable property free of cost amounted to nothing less than a stealthy act of burglary. How was it different in any way from stealing money?

Until then, Labanya had been completely unaware that her image was being worshipped at some secret shrine, away from the public gaze. In a corner of Abanish's library, amidst a cluttered heap of pamphlets and magazines, Shobhan had chanced upon Labanya's photograph, faded from neglect. Having persuaded an artist friend to reproduce the portrait as a drawing, he had returned the photograph to its original place. Like his own shy, secret love, the roses, too, had blossomed in his friend's garden with a natural simplicity; they carried no trace of unlawful presumption. Yet, he had to be punished. With lowered head and scarlet face, wiping away a secret tear, the shy young man took his leave from the house. From afar, Shobhanlal had offered one last instance of self-sacrifice, known only to the Maker. In the B.A. examinations, he had secured the first place and Labanya, the third. That had been a major blow to Labanya's self-esteem. The reasons were twofold: first, that Labanya was often stung by Abanish's deep respect for Shobhan's intellect. The fact that Abanish's respect was combined with special affection only aggravated her suffering. She had tried very hard to surpass Shobhan in their examination results. When Shobhan outshone her nevertheless, it became very difficult for her to forgive him. In her mind remained a lingering suspicion that the difference in marks was the result of Abanish's special tutelage, although Shobhanlal had never sought Abanish's help in preparing for the examinations. For a few days, Labanya would avert her face if Shobhanlal crossed her path. There was no likelihood of her surpassing Shobhan in the M.A. examinations, either. Yet, she defeated him. Abanish himself was surprised. Had Shobhanlal been a poet, he could perhaps have dedicated pages of verse to Labanya; instead, he had sacrificed a large number of examination-marks as an offering to her.

After this, their student days were over. At this juncture, Abanish discovered within himself the agonising truth that even if the heart is stuffed full of learning, the god of love can somehow intrude, and find no dearth of space. Abanish was then forty-seven. At that extremely vulnerable, helpless age, a widow entered his heart, penetrating the protective shield of books in his library, surmounting the high walls of his scholarship. There was no obstacle to their marriage, save Abanish's affection for Labanya. He faced a terrible conflict of desires. He would will himself to study, only to be overpowered by thoughts that were stronger, and more extraordinary. *The Modern Review* would commission a critical article and send him an attractive volume on the history of Buddhist ruins, but he would meditate upon the unpublished book like a Buddhist stupa, weighed down by centuries of silence. The editor would grow impatient, but such is usually the state of a learned man when his scholarship is challenged. When an elephant steps into the quicksand, what chance that it will survive?

At long last, Abanish was troubled by a painful regret. Never having found the time to look beyond his books, he suspected he had failed to notice that his daughter was in love with Shobhanlal, for it would be unnatural for anyone to not love this young man. He grew annoyed with all fathers in general, with himself, and with Nonigopal.

Then came a letter from Shobhanlal. He wanted to borrow a few books from Abanish's library, to write an essay on the history of the Gupta Kingdom, for the Premchand Raichand scholarship examination. '*Have no hesitation*,' was Abanish's prompt and affectionate reply. '*You shall read in my library, as before*.'

Shobhanlal was agitated. He assumed that the eager tone of the letter indicated Labanya's covert consent. He began to frequent the library. On his way in and out of the house, he would sometimes chance upon Labanya, very briefly. Shobhan would then slow his pace. It was his utmost desire that Labanya should say something to him; that she would ask after him, or express some curiosity about the article he was busy writing. If she had, he would have found great relief in opening his notebook to discuss his ideas with Labanya, sometime. He was very eager to know her views on some of his cherished original ideas. But no such conversation took place, nor did he have the courage to force a discussion on her.

Several days passed, in this fashion. It was a Sunday. Shobhanlal had arranged his notebooks on a table, and was turning the pages of a book, taking notes every now and then. The room was deserted, for it was afternoon. Taking advantage of the holiday, Abanish was going somewhere on a visit, he didn't say where. He left instructions that he would not be home for tea.

Suddenly, the door, which had been ajar, was flung open. Shobhanlal's heart gave a sudden jolt. Labanya entered the room. Flustered, Shobhanlal didn't know what to do.

'Why do you come to this house?' demanded Labanya, blazing with fury.

Shobhanlal was too stunned to speak.

'Do you know what your father has said about your visits? Aren't you ashamed of bringing such humiliation upon me?'

'Please forgive me,' pleaded Shobhanlal, with downcast eyes. 'I shall leave at once.'

Without retorting that he was there on Labanya's father's personal invitation, he gathered his books and belongings. His hands trembled violently, a dumb pain beating against his rib-cage. Hanging his head, he left the house.

If one is deprived by some obstacle of the chance to love someone truly loveable, it leads not to indifference but to blind hate, the very obverse of love. Perhaps Labanya, unbeknownst to her, had once awaited a chance to grant Shobhanlal the boon of her love. But Shobhanlal had not approached her in the appropriate way. All subsequent developments went against him. He hurt her most deeply on this last occasion. In her anguish, Labanya utterly misjudged her father. She concluded that it was from a desire to free himself of all obligations that he had summoned Shobhanlal again, hoping to arrange a match between the two of them. This explained her terrible rage against the blameless Shobhanlal.

Labanya now seemed stubbornly determined to ensure that Abanish's marriage took place. Abanish had put aside almost half his savings for his daughter. But after his marriage, Labanya insisted that she would have no part of her patrimony, for she wished to earn her own livelihood.

'I was not keen to marry at all,' protested Abinash, wounded to the quick. 'It was you who obdurately insisted on my marriage. Why do you abandon me now, in this way?'

'I have taken this resolve so that our relationship never deteriorates,' replied Labanya. 'Don't worry, Baba! Grant me your blessings, always, that I may find the path to true happiness.'

She found a job. The entire responsibility for Suroma's education was hers. She could easily have tutored Jati as well, but he would not accept the ignominy of being trained by a female teacher.

Days passed by, in a routine, everyday fashion. Her spare time was stuffed full of English literature, from ancient times to the recent works of Bernard Shaw, and especially the history of ancient Greece and Rome, and the works of Groat, Gibbon, Gilbert and Marr. Whether or not her heart was sometimes ruffled by a restless breeze, I can't say; but her lifestyle left no loophole for any major disruption. At this juncture, disruption arrived in a motor car, driven soundlessly down the middle of the road. Suddenly, the monumental history of Greece and Rome appeared very light; sweeping all else aside, the intensity of the immediate present jolted her consciousness, forcing her awake. Instantly aroused, Labanya at last saw herself as she really was – immersed not in learning, but in pain.

5
Introductions

From the ruins of the past, let us now return to the new constructions of the present.

Leaving Amit in the study, Labanya went in search of Yogamaya. Like a bee at the heart of a lotus blossom, Amit settled into the room. Glancing around, he felt in everything a touch of wistfulness. On the shelves, and on the study table, he saw volumes of English literature. The books seemed to come alive. They had been read by Labanya, their pages turned by her fingers, bearing the trace of her daylong thoughts as her curious eyes travelled over them, books that would lie neglected on her lap on days when she was distracted. He started when he saw the works of John Donne on her table. In his Oxford days, Amit had specialised in the lyrics of Donne and his contemporaries. Today, by a quirk of fate, these same lyrics became the meeting-ground for their hearts.

Like a schoolmaster's textbook, its cover hanging loose from years of use, Amit's life had grown dim, rusted by the prolonged dullness of his days and nights. He had no curiosity about the coming day, and felt no need to greet the present with whole-hearted enthusiasm. But now, he seemed to have landed on a new planet. Here, the pull of gravity was so mild that there was a weightless feeling, like floating above the ground; every moment reached eagerly for the inconceivable; at the touch of the breeze, the body yearned to be a flute; the radiance of the sky suffused his blood, and his innermost being was filled with an excitement like the sap of life that makes a tree blossom. The dusty screen that had veiled his heart was blown away, revealing the extraordinary even in the ordinary. Hence, when Yogamaya slowly entered the room, even this simple act filled Amit with wonder. 'Ah! An apparition, not a mere entrance!' he said to himself.

She was almost forty, but age, instead of slackening her form, had only imparted added dignity. Her fair countenance was full and firm. Her hair was trimmed short, as customary for widows; her benign eyes were full of motherly feeling; her smile was tender. A length of plain, coarse fabric was draped over her head and wrapped around her body. Her bare feet were exquisitely pure. When Amit touched her feet in respectful greeting, he felt as if the blessings of a goddess were coursing through every vein in his body.

'Your *kaka* Amaresh, your father's younger brother, was the most prominent lawyer in our district,' Yogamaya informed him, once introductions were over. 'He had come to our rescue once, when some disastrous litigation had brought us to the brink of bankruptcy. He used to call me *Boudidi*.'

'I am his unworthy nephew,' acknowledged Amit. 'Kaka saved you from bankruptcy, but I have brought you loss. As his *Boudidi* you gained benefits, but as my maternal aunt – my *Mashima* – you will suffer losses.'

'Is your mother still living?' asked Yogamaya.

'She was, once,' replied Amit. 'I should have had a *mashi*, too.'

'Why such longing for a *mashi*, baba?'

'Just think: if I had crashed my mother's car today, there would have been no end to all the scoldings; she would have called it rascally conduct. But if the car were my *mashi*'s, she would laugh at my lack of expertise, taking it for immature behaviour.'

'So let it be your *mashi*'s car, then,' laughed Yogamaya.

Amit darted forward and bent to touch Yogamaya's feet. 'This is why we must believe that we reap the fruit of our deeds from past lives. Born into my mother's lap, I have never striven for the favour of a *mashi*. Crashing a car can't be called a good deed, yet, in a flash, *mashi* descends into my life like a divine boon. Think how many centuries of karma must be behind this occurrence.'

'I wonder whose karma this involves, baba,' laughed Yogamaya. 'Yours, mine, or the motor-mechanic's?'

'Tough question,' acknowledged Amit, running his fingers through his thick locks. 'Karma is not one person's but the whole world's. The stream of karma, flowing from planet to planet through the ages, carrying all their combined influences, has culminated in a collision today, at exactly 9.48 on Friday morning. What will happen next?'

Yogamaya smiled, casting a sidelong glance at Labanya. She had decided upon a match between these two as soon as she was introduced to Amit. With this in mind, she suggested: 'Baba, the two of you could have a chat while I go and attend to your meal.'

Amit could establish a quick rapport with people. '*Mashima* has ordered us to get to know each other,' he began, without any ado. 'Introductions begin with names. Let's get those straight first. You know my name, don't you? My "proper name", as in English grammar.'

'I know you as Amitbabu,' replied Labanya.

'That doesn't work in all situations.'

'Situations may vary, but the subject's name should surely remain the same,' smiled Labanya.

'What you're saying doesn't apply to modern times. If place, time and people can vary, it's unscientific to imagine that names would remain unchanged. I have decided to stake my claim to fame on promoting the 'Relativity of Names'. I would like to inform you at the very outset that for you, my name is not Amitbabu.'

'Do you fancy a western style of address? Mister Roy?'

'That's a remote, overseas sort of name. When determining the distance signified by a name, one should measure the time it takes to travel from the threshold of the ear to the inner chambers of the heart.'

'So, what's this name that travels so swiftly?'

'To increase speed, we must shed some weight. Drop the "babu" from Amitbabu.'

'Not so easy! It will take some time,' answered Labanya.

'The time taken shouldn't be the same for everybody. There's no such thing as uniform time; the pace of a pocket-watch depends on the pocket. That's Einstein's view.'

Labanya rose to her feet. 'Your bath water is turning cold, I'm afraid.'

'I shall accept the cold water with reverence, if you will allow a little more time for introductions.'

'There's no time, I have work to do,' insisted Labanya, and quickly disappeared.

Amit did not proceed immediately for his bath. He savoured in his mind the form of every word as it had taken shape on Labanya's lips, uttered with faint amusement. Amit had seen many beautiful women, but their beauty had the veiled brightness of a full-moon night. Labanya's beauty was like the morning; instead of the allure of mystery, it was suffused with radiant intelligence. While making her a woman, the Creator had added a masculine element to her nature. It was clear at first sight that she had not only the strength to endure suffering, but also the power of intellect. This, for Amit, was her chief attraction. For in Amit's nature, there was intellect, but no mercy; judgement, but no patience; a great deal of knowledge and learning, but no inner peace. In Labanya's countenance, he had glimpsed a peace that did not arise from the contentment of the heart but rested, motionless, in the depths of her intellect.

6
Getting acquainted

Amit was a gregarious person. He could not dwell for long on the beauties of nature. He was accustomed to the sound of his own voice. One couldn't laugh and joke with trees and mountains; any attempt to take liberties with them would boomerang on oneself. Trees and mountains followed their own routine, and expected others to be equally disciplined. In a word, they were humourless. So, away from the city, Amit felt bored and fretful.

But suddenly, the hills of Shillong all around him seemed to fill Amit's heart with zest. Today, he was up before sunrise, quite contrary to his personal religion. From his window, he saw the needles shivering on the deodar trees, against a backdrop of light clouds, upon which the sun, hidden by mountains, had drawn his sweeping, golden brush-strokes. The fiery glow of all these colours left him speechless.

After a quick cup of tea, Amit set out. At that hour, the path was empty. He chose a space under an ancient, mossy pine, and stretched out on the fragrant carpet of pine needles. He lit a cigarette, holding it between his fingers for a long time, without remembering to take a puff.

This forest was on the way to Yogamaya's house. From here, Amit savoured the fragrance of the house, as one breathes in the aroma wafting from the kitchen just before a meal. As soon as his watch signalled a civilised hour, he would go there and demand a cup of tea. At first, evening was the appointed time for his visits there. On the strength of his reputation as a litterateur, he had a standing invitation to join them for discussions. For the first few days, Yogamaya had expressed her enthusiasm for these discussions, until she sensed that Amit's own eagerness was waning as a result. It was not hard to guess that this was due to the use of the plural in place of the dual number. Since then, Yogamaya found frequent reasons to stay away. The slightest probing would have revealed that these occasions for absence were neither unavoidable, nor heaven-decreed, but invented by Yogamaya herself. Evidently, Yogamaya had noticed that these two discussants felt an affection for each other that was considerably deeper than their affection for books. Amit realised that, despite her advanced age, *Mashi* was sharp-eyed, yet tender-hearted. This intensified his enthusiasm for discussion. With the intention of extending the appointed time, he made a mutual arrangement with Jatishankar to help with his English lessons for an hour in the morning and two hours every evening. The help he offered was so excessive that morning would frequently advance into afternoon, and tutelage would slide into aimless talk, until the pressures of civility, coupled with Yogamaya's requests, made it obligatory for him to stay on for lunch. In this way, it became apparent that the call of duty was increasing by the hour.

He was supposed to assist with Jatishankar's lessons at eight in the morning. Normally, he would have considered this an unearthly hour. He used to insist that, for a creature that spends ten months in the womb, the hours of sleep required cannot be measured by the habits of animals and birds. Until now, Amit's nights had encroached upon several hours of his mornings. These stolen hours were best suited for sleep precisely because they were forbidden, he would argue.

But nowadays, he no longer slept soundly. In his heart was an intense eagerness to wake up early. He would awaken needlessly early, and dared not turn over on his side, for fear of oversleeping. Sometimes, he would advance the hands of his watch, something not to be repeated too often, for fear of being caught in the criminal act of stealing time. Today, he glanced at his watch once, and found it was not yet seven. It seemed his watch must have stopped. He held it to his ear to listen to its ticking.

Suddenly, he was startled to see Labanya walking down the road, swinging an umbrella in her right hand. She was dressed in a white sari, with a black, triangular fringed shawl draped across her back. Amit was sure that Labanya, having glimpsed him from the corner of her eye, was nevertheless unwilling to acknowledge his presence by turning her full gaze upon him. As she reached the bend in the road, Amit ran to her side, unable to restrain himself any longer.

'You knew you couldn't avoid me, but still you made me run after you in hot pursuit!' he protested. 'Don't you know how difficult it becomes when you move far away?'

'Difficult? In what way?'

'The unfortunate wretch you've left behind yearns with all his heart to call out to you. But by what name should I call you? With gods and goddesses, it's easy, because they're happy to be addressed by name. Even if you bellow "Durga! Durga!" the ten-armed deity doesn't take offence. But with people such as you, there's a problem.'

'If you don't call me, there will be no problem.'

'When you are near, I manage without any form of address. Therefore I plead, please don't move far away. There is no sorrow greater than being unable to call you even when I yearn to.'

'Why, you're used to English ways.'

'Miss Dutt? That's for the tea-table. Look, the vision of beauty created at the auspicious moment when land and sky came together in the light of dawn, contained within it the name by which heaven and earth call out to each other. Don't you hear that call, resounding in the heavens above, and here below, on earth? In the lives of mortals, too, isn't there a moment for the creation of such a name? Imagine that I have just called out to you, a full-throated cry from the depths of my heart; the name resounds in the forests, and ascends to those brilliant clouds; at the sound of that name, this mountain before us stands lost in thought, its head covered in clouds. Can you ever imagine that name to be Miss Dutt?'

'The naming ritual takes time; meanwhile, let's take a walk,' proposed Labanya, evading the question.

'Human beings take long to learn how to walk, but with me it was just the opposite,' replied Amit, taking the cue from her. 'Since I came here, I have finally learned how to rest. A rolling stone gathers no moss, as they say in English. That's why I was waiting by the wayside before daybreak. So I could glimpse the light of dawn.'

'Do you know the name of that green-winged bird?' asked Labanya, quickly changing the subject.

'Until now, I knew in a general way that the created world includes birds; but I never had the time to discover the special significance of this fact. Strangely enough, since

I came to this place, I have clearly understood that birds indeed exist, and that they even sing.'

'How extraordinary!' laughed Labanya.

'You're laughing at me! I can't remain serious even when I'm being profound. That's a congenital bad habit. The moon, the celestial body that dominates my birth-chart, can never fade away without the flicker of a smile, not even on the dark, deadly night of Krishnachaturdashi.'

'Please don't blame me for feeling amused,' begged Labanya. 'Even the birds would probably burst into laughter if they heard you.'

'Look, people laugh because they fail to grasp my words at first; if they understood my meaning, they'd ponder in silence. It seems a laughing matter that I have learnt to see birds in a new light today. But my words imply a hidden meaning: that today, I see everything in a new light – including myself. That's no laughing matter! Take your-self, for instance: I'm repeating the same idea, but this time, you are speechless.'

'You are not an ancient person, after all,' smiled Labanya. 'You're of very new vintage. Where do you find such enthusiasm to seek out something even newer?'

'In reply to that, I must say something very profound, not suitable for the tea-table. The new element that has entered me is timeless, older than time, ancient as the light of dawn; like the newly-blossomed bhuichampa flower, it is the fresh discovery of something eternal.'

Labanya smiled. She didn't say anything.

'This smile of yours is like the watchman's lantern, meant for spotting thieves,' remarked Amit. 'I realise that my ideas strike you as familiar, for you have encountered them already in your favourite poet's works. I beg you not to brand me a thief. At times my heart, like Sankaracharya, insists that the difference between my writings and someone else's is *maya*, mere illusion. This morning, for instance, it suddenly occurred to me that I should extract from my knowledge of literature a line that would appear to be my own fresh composition, something no other poet could have written.'

'Could you find such a line?' Labanya couldn't help asking.

'Yes.'

'What was it? Please tell me!' begged Labanya, unable to contain her curiosity any longer.

'For God's sake, hold your tongue
and let me love!'

There was a tremor in her heart.

'You must know who wrote that line?' asked Amit, after a long pause.

Labanya slightly inclined her head to indicate assent.

'This line would not have occurred to me if I hadn't discovered the works of John Donne on your table, the other day.'

'You discovered them?'

'It was a discovery, indeed. In bookshops, we glance at books; but on your table, books appear in a new light. When I view the tables in the public library, they seem burdened with books; but when I saw your table, I found it a nesting-place for books. That day, I was able to view the poetry of Donne through the eyes of the spirit. Like paupers at a rich man's funeral, a great crowd of people seem to press against the gates of other poets, But the palace of Donne's verse is solitary, with space enough only for two. That is why I could clearly hear the words that came to me this morning:

> '*For God's sake, hold your tongue
>   and let me love!*'

He had recited these words in Bengali.

'Do you write poetry in Bengali, then?' asked Labanya in surprise.

'I may begin from today, I fear. The old Amit Raye has no idea what the new Amit Raye might do. Perhaps he'll go out to wage war, at this very moment.'

'Wage war? Against whom?'

'That I can't decide. I feel a blind urge to surrender my life to some great cause; the time for regret can follow later.'

'If you must surrender your life, please be cautious,' smiled Labanya.

'Needless to warn me. I'm not willing to step into communal riots. I shall avoid Muslims and Englishmen. If I came across a non-violent, pious-looking elderly person, sounding his motor-horn and driving somewhere in a hurry, I would stand before him, obstruct his path, and demand: "Grant me the gift of war!" I'm referring to the kind of people who visit the hills instead of the hospital to cure their indigestion, shamelessly setting out to savour the air in order to improve their appetite.'

'What if the man drives away, disregarding you?' smiled Labanya.

'Then, I shall raise my hands to the sky and call out after him: "I forgive you this time, for you are my brother; we are children of the same mother – our nation, Mother India, Bharatmata." You see, when we become magnanimous, we can fight, but also forgive.'

'I was frightened when you spoke of waging war, but after your discourse on forgiveness, I feel reassured that I have nothing to fear,' smiled Labanya.

'Will you honour a request of mine?' asked Amit.

'Please tell me what it is.'

'Please don't stay out much longer to improve your appetite, today.'

'Very well, but what next?'

'Let's rest under that tree, where the water trickles by, beneath that rock covered in many-coloured moss.'

'But there's not much time,' protested Labanya, glancing at her watch.

'It is the tragedy of life, Labanya Devi, that time is short. On the desert track, we have with us only half a leather bag of water. We must ensure that it doesn't spill over to be wasted in the dry dust. Punctuality is for those who have plenty of time to spare. God has limitless time at his disposal, hence the sun rises and sets exactly on time. Our tenure is short; it would be prodigal of us to waste time on punctuality. If, at the gates of the celestial city Amaravati, someone were to ask: "What did you accomplish, on earth?" it would be embarrassing to reply, "As I went about my work, I was too busy watching the clock to find time for the contemplation of all those things which transcend the limits of time." That is why I was impelled to invite you to that spot.'

Amit spoke as if there was no possibility of anyone objecting to something to which he himself had no objection. Hence, it was difficult to resist his proposal.

'Let's go,' said Labanya.

In the deep forest shadow, the narrow path descended towards a tribal village. Halfway down, the path was crossed by a small mountain stream, flowing from a waterfall, spreading pebbles to mark its right of way, following its own course in seeming oblivion of the public thoroughfare. Here, the two of them found a place on the rocks. At that spot, water had collected in a hollow crevice, like a green-veiled maiden too timid to appear in public. The very solitude of this spot embarrassed Labanya, for it made her feel exposed. To hide this feeling, she felt like making some trifling remark, but could think of nothing to say. It was like choking in a dream.

'Look, my wise lady,' observed Amit, realising the need to break the silence, 'there are two languages in our land: one formal, the other colloquial. But there should have been yet another language: not the language of society, or of business, but the language of seclusion, meant for places such as this. Like the song of birds and the verse of poets, this language should rise to the throat as readily as sobbing. What a shame that people must rush to bookshops to fulfill this need. Imagine what would happen if we had to rush to the dentist every time we wanted to laugh. Tell me truly, Labanya Devi, don't you feel the urge to voice your thoughts in melody, at this moment?'

Labanya remained silent, her head bent low.

'In the language of the tea-table, there's no end to nice determinations of what's civilised and what isn't. But here, there is nothing either civilised or uncivilised. So what's the solution? It has become necessary to recite a poem. Prose takes very long, but we don't have so much time to spare. If you permit me, I shall begin.'

She had to permit him, for it would be embarrassing to refuse.

'Perhaps you like the poems of Robi Thakur,' said Amit, by way of introduction.

'Yes, I do.'

'I don't. So, please forgive me. I have a favourite poet. His writings are of such high quality that very few people read them. In fact, nobody even considers him significant enough to be condemned. I would like to recite his poems.'

'Why are you so scared?'

'My experience in this matter has been distressing. To criticise the great poet is to be shunned as an outcaste by all of you; to ignore him would also invite harsh words. All the bloodshed in this world has to do with my fancying what others may dislike.'

'Have no fear. I'll cause no bloodshed. I don't seek the approval of others in support of my own taste.'

'Well said. So let us fearlessly begin:

'O *unknown! How can you evade my grasp*
Until I come to know you?

'Do you notice the subject? The bondage of not knowing. It is the harshest bond. Imprisoned in an unknown world, one must get to know it in order to find release: that's the philosophy of liberation.

56

'At what blind moment,
Between sleep and wakefulness,
As night gave way to dawn,
Did I glimpse your face?
I met your gaze, and asked:
In what corner of self-forgetting
Do you hide?

'There's no corner more obscure than the point where you forget yourself. All the precious things in the world that one could never glimpse have vanished into the corner of self-forgetting. But one can't give up hope for that reason.

'Getting to know you
Will not be easy, not like
Whispering sweet nothings.
Your shy, hesitant speech I'll conquer,
Dragging you with rampant force
From fear, shame and doubt,
Into the pitiless light.

'He doesn't give up. What power. Do you see the virility of the writing?

'In a flood of tears you'll awaken,
And know yourself at once.
Your shackles will be broken;
In your freedom, I shall find mine.

'You won't detect quite this tenor in your famous writer's work, for it's like a fire-storm in the sun's atmosphere. These are not mere lyrics: they are life's cruel philosophy.'

Fixing his gaze on Labanya's face, he recited:

> *'O unknown!*
> *Day's done: 'tis dusk; no time remains.*
> *Let a sudden blow destroy*
> *Our fetters. Let knowledge of you*
> *Set me aflame. To that fire*
> *I yield my life, a prayer offering.'*

As soon as his recitation came to an end, Amit grasped Labanya's hand. She gazed at him wordlessly, without withdrawing her hand.

Now, there was no need for words. Labanya forgot even to look at her watch.

7
Matchmaking

'*Mashima*, I'm here to do some matchmaking,' announced Amit to Yogamaya. 'Don't be parsimonious when it's time to pay my dues.'

'Only if I like the proposal. Let's begin with the name, background and physical description of the candidate.'

'The candidate's name doesn't indicate his worth.'

'Then some deductions must be made from the match-maker's dues, it seems.'

'That's an unfair thing to say. A person with a well-known name spends less time at home, more outside. He's busy keeping up appearances in public, instead of maintaining peace on the domestic front. The wife gets a very tiny share of her husband's attention, not enough for complete fulfillment in marriage. The marriage of a well-known man is a partial, inadequate thing, as much to be condemned as polygamy.'

'Very well, so he is not eminent by name. What about his appearance?'

'I'm reluctant to describe him, lest I exaggerate.'

'Must he be marketed only through hyperbole?'

'When selecting a candidate for marriage, two things must be kept in mind – the groom's name should not outshine the reputation of the bride's family, nor should his beauty exceed the bride's.'

'Very well, let's forget his name and appearance. Tell us the rest.'

'The rest, in a nutshell, could be called substance. Well, the man does not lack substance.'

'What about intelligence?'

'He has intelligence enough to be mistaken for a clever man.'

'Learning?'

'Like Newton himself. He knows that he has merely gathered pebbles at the shore of the sea of knowledge. But unlike Newton, he doesn't have the courage to declare this, lest others take him seriously.'

'I can see that the candidate's list of accomplishments is rather short.'

'It was to reveal the full glory of Annapurna that Shiva assumed the role of a beggar. It's nothing to be ashamed of.'

'Then explain the candidate's identity a little more clearly.'

'The family is known to you. The candidate's name is Amitkumar Ray. Why do you laugh, *Mashima*? Do you take this for a joke?'

'I do feel anxious, baba, that it may ultimately turn out to be a joke.'

'To harbour such a suspicion is to cast aspersions upon the candidate.'

'Baba, the ability to laugh away the worries of this world is no mean gift.'

'*Mashi*, the gods have this ability, which is why they are unworthy of marriage. This was something Damayanti had realised.'

'Do you really like my Labanya?'

'How would you like to verify that?'

'The only test would be, for you to know for certain that Labanya is entirely in your hands.'

'Please explain a little more clearly.'

'The true jeweller is one who understands the real value of a jewel, even if it is cheaply bought.'

'*Mashima*, you refine the argument too much. As if you're polishing the psychology of some short story. But the matter itself is extremely coarse: as per the custom of this world, a gentleman is eager to marry a lady. In his personal qualities, the young man would pass muster; as for the young lady, she is beyond description. In such a situation, the ordinary *mashimas* of this world would naturally be overjoyed, and instantly begin to thresh rice on the *dhenki*, to prepare celebratory wedding-sweets.'

'Have no fear, baba, my foot is already on the *dhenki* pedal. You may assume that Labanya is yours. If your desire for her remains intense, even after you have her in your possession, only then would I regard you as a worthy match for such a girl.'

'Your words dazzle even an ultra-modern person like me.'

'What signs of modernity do you find in my words?'

'I find that twentieth-century *mashimas* are afraid even to arrange a marriage.'

'That's because the girls married off by *mashimas* of earlier centuries were dolls, mere playthings. The marriageable girls of today are not interested in fulfilling their mashimas' game-plans.'

'Have no fear. To have is not to possess completely; rather, it increases one's desire. Amit Raye was born into this world only to demonstrate this truth, by marrying Labanya. Why else would my motor car, an inanimate thing, bring about such a bizarre mishap in the wrong place, at the wrong time?'

'Baba, your words have not yet acquired the ring of maturity expected in a person of marriageable age; I hope this won't turn out to be a case of child-marriage.'

'Mashima, my mind has a specific gravity of its own, causing even the heavy words of my heart to float lightly to my lips. But that doesn't reduce the weight of what I say.'

Yogamaya went away, to supervise kitchen chores. Amit wandered from room to room, but failed to glimpse anyone worth seeing. Encountering Jatishankar, he remembered that a lesson on *Antony and Cleopatra* had been scheduled for that morning. From Amit's expression, Jati sensed that it was his duty to take the day off, out of sheer human kindness.

'Amitda,' he pleaded, 'if you don't mind, I'd like the day off to visit Upper Shillong.'

'Those unable to take time off from their studies merely read, without digesting their lessons,' responded Amit, delighted. 'Why harbour such impossible fears? Would I be offended if you wanted the day off?'

'Tomorrow being Sunday, is anyway a holiday. What if you were to imagine…'

'I don't have the mentality of a schoolmaster, my friend. I don't count regular holidays as days off, at all. Enjoying a routine holiday is like hunting a chained beast. It dilutes the joy of taking a break.'

Jati was highly amused, for he sensed the real reason for Amitkumar's enthusiasm in his animated elaboration of the doctrine of holidays.

'Of late, your mind has thrown up all kinds of new ideas about the doctrine of holidays,' he said. 'You had offered me advice the other day, as well. A few more days of this, and I'll become an expert at taking time out.'

'What advice had I offered, the other day?'

'You had said, "Truancy is one of the greatest human qualities. We must not waste a second in answering its call." With these words, you immediately closed your book and rushed outside. Perhaps an occasion for truancy had presented itself, somewhere outdoors, though I had failed to notice it.'

Jati was almost twenty. His heart, too, was stirred by the restlessness in Amit's. All along, he had regarded Labanya as a teacher; but today, Amit's behaviour had made him realise that she was a woman.

'That one should be ready for any task that presents itself, is a maxim of high market-value, like a gold sovereign of Akbar's vintage,' laughed Amit. 'But on its obverse, there should be an engraving exhorting us to heroically embrace truancy whenever the occasion arises.'

'These days, your heroism is very much in evidence.'

Amit patted Jati on the back. 'My friend, when your life's almanac announces *Ashtami* – the sacred date when urgent duties must be sacrificed at one stroke – don't be tardy in your goddess-worship. For *Bijoyadashami* – when the prayers must end and the goddess' image destroyed – arrives soon after.'

Jati departed. Amit's urge for truancy was acute, but there was no sign of the one who inspired truancy. Amit stepped outside.

The climbing rose was in full bloom, flanked on one side by a host of sunflowers, and on the other, by chrysanthemums in square wooden flowerpots. At the top of a grassy slope was a giant eucalyptus tree. Reclining beneath it, leaning against the tree trunk was Labanya. She was wrapped in a grey shawl, sunning her feet in the morning sun. A handkerchief in her lap held a few scraps of bread and some walnut fragments. She had planned to spend the morning feeding the creatures of this world, but had forgotten all about it. Amit came up close; raising her head, Labanya gazed at him in silence, a gentle smile suffusing her countenance. He faced her directly.

'There's good news. I have *Mashima*'s consent.'

Without offering any reply, Labanya cast a walnut fragment at a peach tree that bore no fruit. Instantly, a squirrel ran down the tree trunk. It was one of the creatures awaiting Labanya's charity.

'If you don't mind, I'll shorten your name a bit,' proposed Amit.

'Shorten it, then.'

'I shall call you *Banyo*, the wild one.'

'*Banyo*!'

'No, no, this name might ruin your reputation. Such a name is more appropriate for me. I shall call you *Banya* – the flood. What do you say?'

'Call me by that name, then, but not in your Mashima's presence.'

'Never! Such names are like the root mantra, never to be disclosed to anyone. This name is for my lips and your ears only.'

'Very well.'

'But I, too, need an unofficial name of the same kind. I wonder whether "Brahmaputra" would do. *Banya*, a sudden flood, bursting the banks of the river to make her entry.'

'The name is too weighty for everyday use.'

'You're quite right. One would need a porter to carry such a name. Why don't you give me a name, then? It will be your creation.'

'Fine. I, too, shall shorten your name. I'll call you *Mita*, my intimate friend.'

'Wonderful! In the romantic verses of the Padavali, the name has a double – "Bandhu". *Banya*, I think you could address me by that name in public: what harm in that?'

'What's precious to one person may be cheapened if heard by many. That's my fear.'

'That's not untrue. What, between two people, signifies an intact whole becomes fragmented if it reaches the ears of many. *Banya*!'

'Yes, *Mita*?'

'If I write verses to you, do you know what word would rhyme with your name? "Ananya", the unique!'

'What would that signify?'

'It would signify that you are what you are, and nothing else.'

'That's nothing extraordinary.'

'What do you mean? It's extraordinary, indeed. Rarely do we come across a person who startles us into acknowledging that she is entirely like herself, not like everyone else. In verse, I would put it like this: O my *Banya*, you are *Ananya*, Glorified in your own being.'

'Would you write poetry, then?'

'Sure. Who can stem the flow of my verse?'

'Why this desperation?'

'Let me explain. Last night I stayed up till two-thirty, flipping through the pages of *The Oxford Book of Verse*, just like someone tossing and turning sleeplessly. I couldn't locate any love-poems at all, though earlier I used to stumble upon them at every step. The world is clearly waiting, today, for me to take up my pen.'

With these words, he grasped Labanya's left hand in both of his. 'My hands are joined with yours, so how would I hold my pen?' he asked. 'The finest form of union is a meeting of hands. No poet could match in writing the ease with which your fingers communicate with mine.'

'You don't like anything easily; that's why I fear you so much, *Mita*!'

'But try to understand what I'm saying. Rama tried to test Sita's purity with external fire; that's why he lost her. But the purity of verse is tested by the fire of the heart. If a person lacks this fire in his heart, how would he undergo such an ordeal? He would have to rely on the opinion of others, which very often is abusive. Today, my heart is aflame; when I test all my previous reading in the light of that fire, how little survives! Most of it burns instantly to ashes in the roaring flames. Today, I stand in the midst of all those noisy poets, and find myself forced to plead: "Don't shout! Speak the truth quietly:

'For God's sake, hold your tongue
and let me love!'"'

For a long time, the two of them remained silent. Then, Amit raised Labanya's hand to stroke his face.

'Just think, *Banya*,' he said, 'today, at this very moment, what countless numbers across the world experience the same sense of yearning, but how few will find fulfilment!

I am one of those very few. Only you, of all the people in this world, spotted this fortunate man under this eucalyptus tree in a remote corner of the Shillong hills. It's the extraordinary things of this world that remain extremely understated, elusive to the eye. Yet the hollow noise of crooked politics raises its fist at the great void, and its shout echoes all the way from Goldighi in Kolkata to Noakhali and Chittagong. This utterly worthless news makes headlines all over Bengal. Who knows, perhaps it's for the best!'

'What is?'

'It's best that the things that really matter wander freely in the thoroughfares of everyday life, yet elude the gaze of evil eyes that would hound them to death. They are in tune with the inner pulse of the universe. Tell me, *Banya*, I've been chattering away, but what are you thinking of, so silently?'

Labanya kept her gaze averted. She made no reply.

'Your silence is like dismissing my words without paying any wages,' protested Amit.

'Your words frighten me, *Mita*,' answered Labanya, without raising her eyes.

'What are you afraid of?'

'What is it you want from me, and what can I really offer you? I find it hard to figure out.'

'What you offer requires no thought: that is the value of your offering.'

'My heart quailed when you said Korta-Ma had given her consent. The day seemed near when I must surrender to captivity.'

'Surrender you must.'

'Your tastes and intellect are far superior to mine, Mita. On our journey together, I may one day fall far behind; then you will never turn back to call me. When that happens, I shall not blame you at all. No, no, don't say anything: listen to me first. I beseech you not to ask for my hand in marriage. If we try to undo the knot after we are married, it will only get more tangled. What I have received from you is enough to last me a lifetime. But you must not delude yourself.'

'*Banya*, in today's spirit of largesse, why summon up fears of the miserliness that tomorrow might bring?'

'It is you who empower me to utter the truth, Mita. What I say now is something you already know in your heart of hearts. You don't want to admit it, lest it interfere, ever so slightly, with the pleasure of the moment. You are not meant to lead a settled life; taste is a thirst that drives you to a life of wandering. That's why you frolic in different literary fields, and the same urge draws you to me, as well. Shall I tell you the truth? In your innermost heart, you consider marriage to be what you would call vulgar. It's terribly respectable, the cherished favourite of those god-fearing materialists who use their property and their spouse as an enormous bolster to prop them up.'

'You can say extraordinarily harsh things in an extraordinarily gentle tone, *Banya*.'

'I hope love will always give me the strength to remain firm, *Mita*; may I never falter ever so slightly from a desire to delude you. May you remain exactly as you are, and may you like me only as much as your taste permits. But I will be satisfied only if you don't assume the slightest responsibility.'

'Let me have my say, *Banya*. How amazingly you have analysed my nature! I shall not argue about that. But you are wrong on one count. Human character is also subject to change. In the domesticated state, one's identity is static, bound in chains, as it were. Then, by a sudden stroke of fortune, the shackles are broken, and one's character rushes out into the wilderness to assume a different image.'

'What image have you assumed today?'

'One that doesn't match my usual appearance. I have met many women before this, but that was always on the paved banks of man-made channels, by the lantern-light of taste. Such meetings permit you to see, but not to know. Tell me yourself, *Banya*, is my acquaintance with you of the same order?'

Labanya remained silent.

'When two stars circle each other, exchanging greetings from a distance, their style is quite pleasant and safe, a matching of tastes rather than a union of hearts. But if a sudden deadly encounter takes place, their lanterns are extinguished, and the two stars merge in flames. Such a fire is now ignited, and Amit Raye stands transformed. Such is the history of man. What seems like a stream of continuity is really a string of coincidences. The rhythm of the universe is jolted and jostled along by these coincidences; the ages succeed each other to the uneven beat of the *jhaptaal*. You have altered my rhythm, Banya; a rhythm that binds your music to mine.'

Labanya's eyelashes grew wet. All the same, she couldn't help thinking: 'Amit's mind is of a literary bent, each experience summoning up a fountain of words. This is the harvest of his life, the source of his joy. That's why he needs me. Like a shower of rain, my warmth must melt all the thoughts frozen in his heart, thoughts that weigh him down, though he does not hear them.'

They were silent for a long time.

'Tell me, *Mita*, don't you think Shah Jahan rejoiced in Mumtaz's death when the Taj Mahal was complete?' asked Labanya, suddenly. 'Her death was necessary for his dream to come true. Death was Mumtaz's greatest gift of love. The Taj Mahal is not an expression of Shah Jahan's grief: it's an image of his joy.'

'At every instant, you startle me with your words!' exclaimed Amit. 'You must be a poet.'

'I don't want to be a poet.'

'Why not?'

'To merely light the lamp of words with the fire of life is not what my heart desires. Words suit those born into this world for the express purpose of decorating the festival of life. But my life's warmth is dedicated solely to work.'

'Do you disown words, *Banya*? Don't you know how your words awaken my heart? How would you understand the nature and significance of your utterances? I see it is time to summon up Nibaran Chakrabarti again. You are tired of hearing his name repeated so often. But how can I help it, when the man acts as custodian of my heart's innermost thoughts? Nibaran has not yet grown tired of himself; every time he writes a poem, it's his first, a new beginning. The other day, leafing through his notebooks, I chanced upon a piece he wrote not so long ago. It's a poem about a waterfall. How did he discover that

I have found my own waterfall here in the Shillong hills?
He writes:

   '*O waterfall! In your stream, so pure and clear,*
   The sun and stars see their image appear.

'Had I been a writer, I could not have described you more clearly. You have a transparent quality that easily mirrors the brightness of the sky. I glimpse that all-suffusing radiance in your countenance, your smile, your words, your stillness when at rest and your movement as you walk down the path.

   '*Today, upon your water's edge,*
      Let my shadow sometimes play,
   And with that shadow, smiling, merge
      The cheerful babble of your voice.
   Grant me speech, for you possess
      The gift of speech eternal.

'You are the waterfall, not merely flowing with the current of life, but also matching your speech with your movement. Your flow strikes chords of music even from the hard, immobile rocks of this world.

   '*My shadow and your laughter*
      In one image converge,
   Arousing within my soul
      A wild poetic urge.
   Moment by moment, in rhythmic motion,
      Your sparkle stirs my soul to words.

O waterfall! I saw myself today
As word made flesh.
In your flow my heart awakens
And I recognise myself.'

'For all my sound and light, your shadow remains but a shadow. I can't hold it captive,' observed Labanya, with a wan smile.

'But you may find, one day, that when all else is gone, I shall remain personified in words,' replied Amit.

'Where?' smiled Labanya. 'In the notebooks of Nibaran Chakarabarty?'

'That wouldn't be surprising. The subterranean stream that flows within my heart somehow emerges into public view as Nibaran's waterfall.'

'Then perhaps, someday, I may find your heart in Nibaran Chakrabarti's fountain, and nowhere else.'

At this moment, they were summoned to the house for their morning repast.

'Labanya wants to see everything clearly by the light of her intellect,' mused Amit, on the way. 'She can't forget herself even at moments when people would naturally wish to forget themselves. I can't refute what Labanya has said, after all. We must express the deepest ideas of one's innermost soul. Some of us achieve this in the way we live our lives, and some of us through creativity – touching life, yet withdrawing from it, just as a river constantly moves away from its shores as it flows. Shall I always move away from life, carried away by the flow of my writings? Is this the difference between men and women? Men devote their entire energy to create something that loses itself at every step in the cause of its own progress. Women devote their whole energy to preserve and protect, blocking the path of new creation only to sustain the past. Innovation is the enemy of the conservative; the conservative obstructs the path of creation. Why should it be so? They are bound to clash at some point. Intense affinity is usually accompanied by great animosity. Which leads me to believe that liberation, not union, is our greatest goal.'

The thought pained Amit, but his heart could not reject the idea.

8
Labanya's Argument

'Labanya, my girl, have you understood the situation correctly?' Yogamaya wanted to know.

'I have understood it correctly, Ma.'

'Amit is very restless, I must admit. That's why I'm so fond of him. Don't you see how disorganised he is? As if he has butter-fingers: things seem to keep slipping from his grasp.'

'If he indeed had to keep a grip on things, if matters didn't keep slipping out of his grasp, he would find it difficult,' smiled Labanya. 'Not to possess what becomes his own, or to lose a thing as soon as he owns it – such is the law of his life. It doesn't suit his nature to keep what he gets.'

'Truth be told, my child, I really enjoy his childish behaviour.'

'That's the way with mothers. When it comes to childish behaviour, the mother takes all the responsibility, while the son's actions are ascribed to mere playfulness. But why do you ask me to become a burden on someone who cannot take responsibility?'

'Don't you see, Labanya, his wayward mind seems to have grown much more tranquil of late. I feel very sorry for him. Whatever you may say, he does love you.'

'He does, indeed.'

'Then why worry?'

'I don't want to wound his nature by inflicting even the slightest torment upon it, Korta Ma.'

'To the best of my knowledge, Labanya, love demands

a degree of torment, and inflicts a degree of torment as well.'

'Korta Ma, such forms of torment have their own grounds; but a threat to one's nature is unbearable. The more I read the literature of love, the more strongly I'm convinced that the tragedy of love occurs whenever people fail to accept their mutual independence, when they impose their will unjustly on others, when they imagine that we can change people, re-create them to suit our own desires.'

'Well, my girl, if two people are to set up house together, it's impossible not to re-create each other to some extent. Where there's love, such re-creation is easy; where love is missing, the attempt to hammer people into shape brings about what you describe as tragedy.'

'Forget those who are born for domesticity. They are made of ordinary mortal clay, moulded and beaten into shape by the pressures of everyday life. But those who are not made of mortal clay at all can never relinquish their independence. A woman who fails to understand this feels ever more deprived, the more insistently she asserts her claims upon her partner. The man who fails to understand this increasingly loses touch with the real person, the more he tries to dominate her. I'm convinced that, in most cases, what we call fulfillment is nothing but the touch of handcuffs on the wrist.'

'What do you want to do, Labanya?'

'I don't want my marriage to become a cause for sorrow. Marriage is not for everyone. Do you know, Korta Ma, people with a finicky nature accept others selectively, choosing the qualities they like, rejecting what they dislike in a person. But when trapped in marriage, men and women come too close; in the absence of separate spaces, it becomes necessary to deal with the whole person, from very close quarters. It's no longer possible to conceal any part of oneself.'

'You don't know yourself, Labanya. For you to gain acceptance, no part of your nature need be excluded.'

'But it's not me he wants. I don't think he has ever glimpsed my everyday, home-loving self. At my touch, his heart instantly erupts into a nonstop flood of words. With those words, he has merely constructed an image of me. If his heart grows tired, if he runs out of words, then in the ensuing silence will emerge a very ordinary woman, not of his own creation. Marriage forces one to accept people as they are; there's no room for the creation of imagined forms.'

'Do you feel that Amit can't entirely accept even a woman like you?'

'He can, if he changes his nature. But why should he change? I wouldn't want that.'

'What do you want?'

'To remain, as long as possible, a dream that lives in his words, and in the playfulness of his heart. And why call it a dream? It's a special incarnation of my self, a special form, which manifests itself as a reality within a special world. So what if it's a short-lived, many-hued butterfly newly emerged from its cocoon, what harm in that? It's not as if a butterfly is less real than anything else in this world. So what if it appears at sunrise and dies at sunset? We must only ensure that this short lifespan should not have been in vain.'

'Let us assume that Amit will only find you a short-lived enchantment. But what about you? Do you not wish to marry? Is Amit, too, a mere infatuation for you?'

Labanya remained silent, offering no reply.

'When you argue, I can see that you are a very well-read young lady,' said Yogamaya. 'I can neither think like you, nor speak like you. What's more, I probably can't act with the same firmness. But I've also observed you through the chinks in your argument, my child. The other night – it was about midnight – I noticed a light in your room. Entering, I found you bent over your table in tears, your face hidden in your hands. The girl I saw was not a scholar of philosophy. I had a brief urge to comfort you; then I thought: every woman must weep when it's time for tears, no use trying to suppress anything. I know very well that you want to love, not to create. If you can't devote yourself to service with all your heart and soul, how will you live? That's why I insist, you can't do without him. Don't take a sudden vow of spinsterhood. I'm apprehensive because it's hard to change your mind once you've taken a stubborn decision.'

Labanya remained silent, needlessly pleating the end of her sari in her lap.

'I have often thought, looking at you, that your minds have grown too refined, from so much reading and thinking,' continued Yogamaya. 'Our world is unworthy of the ideas that have secretly taken shape in your minds. It appears that you wouldn't spare even the inner light of the mind which remained hidden in our times. This light seems to pierce through the coarse fabric of the body, rendering it invisible. In our times, the simple emotions of the heart were enough to create the joys and sorrows of our world, and even then, the problems we faced were not inconsiderable. Today, you've carried things to such an extreme, all of you, that nothing remains simple anymore.'

Labanya gave a faint smile. Just the other day, Amit had been explaining to Yogamaya about the invisible light of the intellect; that was the source of her argument – and it was a refined argument, too. Mathakrun, Yogamaya's mother, wouldn't have understood such ideas.

'In the course of time, Korta Ma, the more clearly the human mind begins to understand everything, the more staunchly it can withstand the impact of such knowledge. The fear and the sorrow of living in darkness are intolerable, because you can't see clearly in the dark.'

'I feel now that it would have been better if the two of you had never met.'

'No, no, don't say that. I can't even imagine that things could have turned out any differently. It was once my firm conviction that I was utterly dull and uninteresting, that I would spend my life merely reading books and passing examinations. Now I have suddenly realised that I'm capable of love, as well. It's enough for me, that something so impossible should have become a possibility in my life. I feel as if, having remained a shadow all these days, I have now become a real person. What more can I desire? Please don't ask me to marry, Korta Ma.'

With these words, she flung herself on the ground, hid her face in Yogamaya's lap, and burst into tears.

9
Change of Abode

At first, everyone had assumed that Amit would be back in Kolkata in a fortnight. Noren Mitter had laid a heavy wager that he wouldn't stay away longer than a week. A month went by, then two months, but there was no sign of Amit. His stay at the apartment in Shillong was over. Some zamindar from Rangpur had come to occupy it. After much hunting, lodgings were found close to Yogamaya's residence. It was once home to a milkman or a gardener, before it fell into the hands of a clerk, who had given it a touch of shabby gentility. The clerk, too, was now dead; his widow rented out the lodgings. Due to the scarcity of doors and windows, the room offered little scope for the free play of light, air and space, the three elements; but on rainy days, water, the fourth element, descended with unforeseen plenitude, penetrating through unseen openings.

One day, seeing the condition of the room, Yogamaya was shocked. 'Baba, why subject yourself to such an ordeal?' she demanded.

'Uma undertook the penance of starvation, giving up even a diet of leaves in the end. Mine is the penance of dispossession: giving up bed, table, chairs, I am down to the bare walls, almost. That other event took place in the Himalaya mountains; this one has happened in the mountains of Shillong. There, the bride desired a groom; here, the groom longs for a bride. There, Narad played matchmaker, but here, we have Mashima herself. Now, if Kalidasa ultimately fails to make an appearance, I'll have to play his role as well, as best I can.'

Amit spoke these words in jest, but they pained Yogamaya. She was about to say, 'Come and stay with us,' but stopped herself in time. The Maker has brought a crisis into being, she thought; my intervention could cause impossible complications. She sent across a few items from her own house. Meanwhile, her sympathy for this hapless youth grew doubly strong.

'Labanya, my child, don't harden your heart,' she pleaded repeatedly.

One day, after a heavy downpour, Yogamaya went to enquire after Amit, to find him crouching alone on a blanket under a rickety table, reading an English book. Finding that raindrops had unrestricted access to random areas of the room, Amit had ensconced himself in a cave-like shelter under the table. At first he laughed heartily at himself, then turned his attention to literary criticism. His mind raced to Yogamaya's residence, but his body proved an obstacle. For, having bought an expensive raincoat in Kolkata, where such an item was redundant, he had forgotten it when he left for this place where it was a constant necessity. He had brought an umbrella, which he had most probably left behind at his chosen destination, unless it was lying beneath that old deodar tree.

'What's the matter, Amit!' exclaimed Yogamaya, as soon as she entered.

'My room today is struck by a wild, raving lunacy; its condition is not much better than mine,' explained Amit, hurrying out from under the table.

'Raving lunacy?'

'Meaning, the ceiling is almost like the Indian nation. The links between its parts have come loose. So, an onslaught from above causes a random downpour of tears everywhere; and a storm that strikes from without raises the hiss of deep sighs. By way of protest, I have raised a scaffold above my head, an example of peaceful home rule amidst the misgovernment of this entire room. This demonstrates a basic law of politics.'

'What's this basic law, let's hear.'

'Namely, that even the haphazard arrangements of the poor tenant who occupies the house are better than the rule of an absentee landlord, however powerful he might be.'

Yogamaya now felt very annoyed with Labanya. The deeper her affection for Amit became, the higher he rose in her esteem. 'Such learning, such intellect, so many degrees and qualifications, and yet, such a simple heart! What an extraordinary ability to put things neatly in words! And speaking of personal appearance, he is much more beautiful to my eyes than Labanya. It's Labanya's good fortune that, under some special planetary influence, Amit has found her so enchanting. And for Labanya to cause such suffering to this excellent young man! To simply announce, upon a whim, that she will not marry! As if she's some royal empress! As if she's Sita, vowing to marry only the man who can break the fabled bow. Such arrogance will do her no good. The wretched girl is condemned to die of grief.'

Yogamaya thought, once, of driving Amit to her own residence. Then, an idea occurred to her.

'Wait a bit, baba, I'm just coming,' she told him.

Back in her own house, she spotted Labanya reclining on the sofa in her room, her feet wrapped in a shawl, immersed in Gorky's *Mother*. Yogamaya's temper flared at the sight of such comfort.

'Come, let's go for a drive,' she proposed.

'Korta Ma, I don't feel like going out today.'

Yogamaya didn't realise that Labanya had sought refuge in this work of fiction, in an attempt to escape from herself. All afternoon, ever since she finished lunch, she awaited Amit's arrival in a state of restless anticipation. Her heart kept telling her that he would arrive at any moment. The pine trees outside were stirred by the playful breeze from time to time, and in the heavy downpour, the mountain springs that had newly sprung to life were overactive, as if racing breathlessly against the short span of their life. A restless desire grew within Labanya, to break all barriers, discard all hesitation, and, grasping Amit's hands in her own, to declare: 'For ever and ever, in this life and the next, I am yours!' Today, it was easy to make such a declaration. The whole sky was full of desperate bravado, calling out some unknown message carried in gusts of wind. The language of the sky had awakened the wilderness to words; covered in torrents of rain, the mountain peaks stood waiting to hear the voice of the sky. If only someone would wait upon Labanya's words in just the same way, enormous, silent, with open-hearted attention! But hour upon hour had passed, and no-one appeared. Gone was the auspicious moment for uttering the secrets of her heart! If someone were to approach her afterwards, she would be at a loss for words; her mind, then, would be full of doubt, and the resounding war-cry of god in his dance of destruction would have faded from the sky. The years pass in silence; then one day, at some special hour, speech comes knocking at one's door. If one fails, at that moment, to find the key to unlock the door, never again can one receive the divine power to utter the truth without embarrassment. The day such power of speech arrives, one feels like announcing to the whole world: 'Listen, all of you! I am in love!' 'I am in love!' These words, like some unknown bird flying across the seas, have travelled so far, over such a long time! It was for these words that divinity had waited within my heart, all these days. At the touch of these words, today, my entire life, my whole world, grows pure and true. Her face hidden in her pillow, Labanya cried importunately, to some unknown person: 'Truth, truth, there is no truth greater than this!'

Time passed, but the awaited visitor did not arrive. Labanya's heart ached with the burden of anticipation. She stepped into the veranda to wet her body with splashes of rain. Then a deep languor came over her heart, filling it with intense despair. It seemed as if the spark of life had been ignited in a single flash of fire, only to be extinguished forever, leaving the future blank. She lost the courage to accept Amit completely on the strength of her inner faith. The strong faith aroused in her heart just a while ago, had now dwindled. After lying in silence for a long time, she reached for the book on her table. It took some time for her to focus on the story; then, without being aware of it, she entered the flow of the narrative and forgot herself.

At this juncture, Yogamaya invited her for a drive, but she felt no enthusiasm.

Yogamaya drew up a chair and fixed her shining eyes on Labanya's face. 'Come, tell me the truth, Labanya. Do you love Amit?'

Labanya started up. 'Why do you ask such things, Korta Ma?'

'If you don't love him, why don't you tell him clearly? It is cruel of you; if you don't want him, then don't hold him captive.'

Labanya's heart was heaving, but no words rose to her lips.

'I just saw him in such a sorry state, my heart breaks for him. For whose sake does he languish here like a beggar? Don't you realise at all how fortunate is the woman such a boy desires?'

'Do you ask about my love, Korta Ma?' exclaimed Labanya, struggling to overcome the lump in her throat. 'I can't imagine anyone in this world to be more in love than I. I could die for love. All that I have been, through all these years, has evaporated. For me, this is a new beginning, a beginning without end. How can I explain to anyone how extraordinary is this transformation within myself? Has anyone ever known such a state of mind?'

Yogamaya was astonished. She had always noted a deep tranquility about Labanya. Where had this intolerable agony concealed itself, all these years?

'Labanya, my child,' she gently coaxed, 'don't suppress your true self. Amit is searching for you in the dark. Reveal yourself fully to him, without any fear. If the light ignited within you could light a spark in him as well, then he would not lack for anything. Come my child, come with me. Let's proceed immediately.'

They headed for Amit's lodgings, the two of them together.

10
The Second Stage

Amit was perched on a stack of newspapers, placed on the damp seat of his chair. He was writing at the table, a pile of foolscap paper by his side. At that very moment, he was embarking on his famous autobiography. When asked the reason why, he would reply that his life, at this moment, had suddenly taken on a many-hued brilliance, like the hills of Shillong when the clouds part at dawn. How could he refrain from expressing his new-found awareness of the value of his own existence? According to Amit, biographies are written after the subject's death for then, though the world takes one for dead, one lives again, intensely, in the minds of men. It was Amit's feeling that, during his stay in Shillong, he had experienced a death of sorts, his past vanishing like a mirage, while in another sense, he had become vibrantly alive. Against the dark backdrop of the past, a radiant vision had appeared. It was necessary to place this revelation on record. For few in the world are fortunate enough to experience such a thing; like a bat nesting in a cave, most people spend their life, from birth to death, in a kind of twilight gloom.

It was drizzling. The stormy wind had died down, the clouds had lightened.

'How unfair, *Mashima*!' exclaimed Amit, rising to his feet.

'Why, baba, what have I done?'

'I'm completely unprepared for this visit. What will Shrimati Labanya think?'

'We need to give Shrimati Labanya some food for thought. When we seek to know something, it's best to be acquainted with all the facts. Why should that give *Srijukta* Amit cause for worry?'

'It's best for the *Shrimati* to be acquainted with facts about the *Srijukta's* wealth. As for the poverty of the "Sriheen", or the hapless one, knowledge of it is meant for you, my *Mashima*.'

'Why such discrimination, my child?'

'For my own sake. One must claim riches with riches, and blessings with want. In human civilisation, *devis*, goddesses like Labanya, have given rise to wealth, while the *Mashimas* have provided blessings.'

'The *devi* and the *Mashima* may be one and the same, Amit; there is no need to hide your penury.'

'This must be answered in the language of the poet. To explain what I say in prose, the language of rhyme becomes necessary. Matthew Arnold calls poetry a criticism of life. I would like to amend that to "a commentary on life, in verse". Let me inform my special visitor that the lines I am about to recite are not composed by a famous poet:

'*Seek not your heart's desire*
When your hands are empty,
Nor beg at love's threshold with tear-wet eyes

'Please think about this: love is fulfilment; its desire is not the poverty of the destitute. It is when the Lord loves his devotee that He appears to him in a beggar's guise.

'*We'll exchange garlands when*
You bring a necklace made of gems;
Would you place the deity's shrine
On the empty dust beside the road?

'That's why I asked the goddess to consider before entering my room. What shrine can I devise for you when I have none to offer? These damp newspapers? Nowadays, I am terrified of being stained by editorial ink. As the poet says, I invite the desired one to join me in revelry when the cup of life brims over, not to share my thirst when I'm thirsty.

'*In the blossoming forests of spring,*
Clasp your loved one to your heart
When the lamp of life burns brightly,
A myriad flames shining in the dark.

'In the laps of our *mashis*, we begin the first stage of life's *tapasya* or holy endeavour: a meditation on poverty, the naked ascetic's prayer for affection. The hardships of this hut are meant for such devotional pursuits. I've decided to call this hut the Mashtuto Bungalow, named after my *mashi*.'

'Baba, the second stage of *tapasya* is the pursuit of wealth, a meditation on love, with the goddess beside you as your partner. Even in this hut, your prayers will not be concealed by damp newspapers. Are you trying to delude yourself that a divine boon has been denied you? In your heart of hearts, you must know that the boon has been granted.'

With these words, she stood the two of them side by side, and placed Labanya's right hand on Amit's. Removing the gold chain from Labanya's neck, she used it to bind their hands together. 'May your union be everlasting!' she proclaimed.

Together, Amit and Labanya touched Yogamaya's feet in obeisance.

'Wait here, both of you,' she instructed them. 'I'll fetch some flowers from the garden.'

She drove off in the car to collect the flowers. For a long while, the pair sat side by side on the cot, in silence. Then, raising her face to Amit's, Labanya asked, in a low voice: 'Why did you stay away all day?'

'The reason is so trifling,' replied Amit, 'that it would take courage to mention it on a day such as this. History provides no instance of a lover postponing his rendezvous with the beloved on a cloudy day, for lack of a raincoat. Rather, the books decree that the lover must swim across the fathomless waters. But then, we speak of the history of the innermost heart. Do you imagine I'm not swimming in those waters, too? Can I ever make my way across that shoreless deep?' He proceeded to recite, first in English, then in Bengali:

'*For we are bound where mariner has not yet*
   dared to go,
      And we will risk the ship, ourselves and all.

'Did you wait for me today, Banya?'

'Yes, *Mita*. All day, I seemed to hear your footfall in the sound of the rain. It seemed you were travelling an

90

impossible distance to come to me. But now, at last, you have indeed entered my life.'

'Not knowing you was like a dark abyss at the centre of my life, *Banya*. That was the most hideous part of my existence. Today, that hollow is full to the brim: the light sparkles on it, the entire sky is mirrored in it. Today, that very spot has become the most beautiful part of my existence. These words, pouring out of me, are the sound of waves in the lake that fills my heart. There is no stopping them now.'

'What were you doing all day, *Mita*?'

'You reposed, motionless, at the centre of my heart. I wanted to say something to you, but where were the words? The rain came down from the skies, and I kept pleading, give me words, give me words!' He recited, in English and then in Bengali:

> 'O, *what is this?*
> *Mysterious and uncapturable bliss*
> *That I have known, yet seems to be*
> *Simple as breath and easy as a smile,*
> *And older than the earth.*

'That is what I do. I take the words of others, and make them my own. If I had the gift of music, I would set Vidyapati's rain-song to a tune, and make it completely my own:

> 'Vidyapati *wonders, how shall I pass*
> *My days and nights without Hari?*

'How can I pass day after day in the absence of the person I cannot live without? Where can I find the right tune for this particular idea? I gaze heavenwards, pleading, sometimes, "Give me words!" and sometimes, "Give me music!" The deity even descends to earth, bearing words and music, but somewhere along the way, he mistakes someone else for me, and offers his gift randomly to another – perhaps to that Robi Thakur of yours.'

'Even the admirers of Robi Thakur don't remember him as frequently as you do!' laughed Labanya.

'*Banya*, I'm a little too garrulous today, am I not? A monsoon shower of words has descended upon my heart. If you keep track of the weather-report, you will note the countless inches of madness I've been notching up, each day. Had I been in Kolkata, I would have burned out the tyres of my car to rush you to Moradabad. If you were to ask, "Why Moradabad?" I would have no reason to offer, none whatsoever. When the flood is upon us, it babbles, rushes on, and carries time along with it in frothy tide of laughter.'

At this juncture, Yogamaya brought in a basketful of sunflowers. 'Labanya, my girl, offer these flowers at his feet, today,' she advised.

This was nothing but a womanly attempt to produce, through ritual, an outward, concrete form for what lay concealed in the recesses of the heart. Women have an innate desire to create immanent form by giving things a material, bodily shape.

'*Banya*, I want to offer you a ring,' whispered Amit to Labanya.

'Why, *Mita*, what is the need?' she asked.

'I can't begin to fathom the immensity of the gift you have offered me today, in giving me your hand. Poets harp on about the beloved's face. But how much of the heart's language is signalled through the hand! All the fondness of love, all its dedication, all the tenderness of the heart, all the unutterable words – the hand conveys all! The ring will encircle your finger, like a tiny little statement from me. What I wish to say is only this: "I have found you!" Why not let this utterance of mine adorn your hand in the language of gold and gemstones?'

'Very well,' said Labanya.

'I'll order it from Kolkata. Tell me, which precious stone do you like?'

'I want no stone, just a single pearl.'

'Fine, that's a good idea. I, too, am fond of pearls.'

11
Love's Philosophy

The wedding was fixed for the month of Agrahayan. Yogamaya would travel to Kolkata to make all the arrangements.

'You were to have left for Kolkata long ago,' Labanya reminded Amit. 'You spent your days in a state of uncertainty, but now you're free. You may depart with a mind free of doubt. We shall not meet again until the time of our wedding.'

'Why such harsh discipline?'

'To sustain the simple joy you spoke of the other day.'

'These are words spoken from deep knowledge. The other day, I suspected you were a poet, but today, I suspect you're a philosopher. Well said, indeed! To keep simple things simple, one must be harsh. If you want your verse to have an easy rhythm, you must fix the caesura firmly in the right place. I am so greedy, my mind resists marking a pause at any point in the poem of my life. The rhythm is broken, and life, lacking pace, becomes bondage. Very well, I shall depart tomorrow, abruptly cutting short these days of fulfilment. It will be like that line in the epic about Meghnad's death, a line that seems to have stopped short in amazement:

'*When you departed for hell*
Untimely!

'I may go away from Shillong, but the month of Agrahayan can't suddenly slip away from the almanac! Do you know what I shall do in Kolkata?'

95

'What will you do?'

'While *Mashima* makes arrangements for the wedding, I must prepare for the days that are to follow. People forget that conjugal life is an art, to be created anew each day. Do you remember, *Banya*, how King Aja had described Indumati in *Raghuvamsha*?'

'My favourite pupil has artistry in her blood,' quoted Labanya.

'Such artistry of the blood belongs to conjugal life,' declared Amit. 'Barbarians generally imagine the wedding ceremony to be the real moment of union, which is why the idea of union is often so utterly neglected afterwards.'

'Please explain the art of union as you imagine it in your heart. If you want me to be your disciple, then let today be the first lesson.'

'Very well, then, listen. The poet creates rhythm out of deliberately placed obstructions. Union, too, should be rendered beautiful by means of deliberately placed obstacles. To cheapen a precious thing so that it is to be had for the asking is to cheat your own self. For the pleasure of paying a high price is by no means negligible.'

'Let's hear how the price is to be calculated.'

'Wait! Let me describe what my heart has visualised. Beside the Ganges, there will be a garden-estate on the other side of Diamond Harbour. A small steam-launch would take us to Kolkata and back, within a couple of hours.'

'But why the need to travel to Kolkata?'

'Now there is no need to, please be assured. I do visit the bar-library, not to engage in trade, but to play chess.

The attorneys have realised that I have no need for work, and therefore, no interest in it. When a case comes up, concerning some mutual dispute, they hand me the brief, but nothing more than that. But right after marriage, I'll show you what it means to set to work, not in search of a livelihood, but in search of life. At the heart of the mango lies the seed, neither sweet, nor soft, nor edible; yet the entire mango depends on it, takes shape from it. You understand, don't you, why the stony seed of Kolkata is necessary? To keep something hard at the core of all the sweetness of our love.'

'I understand. In that case, I need it, too. I must also visit Kolkata, from ten to five.'

'What's wrong with that? But it should be for work, and not in order to explore the neighbourhood.'

'What work can I take up, tell me? Without any wages?'

'No, no, a job without wages is neither work nor play: it's mostly all about shirking. If you wish, you can easily become a professor in a women's college.'

'Very well, that shall be my wish. What then?'

'I can visualise it clearly: the shore of the Ganges. From the lowest level of the paved bathing area rises an ancient banyan tree, laden with aerial roots. While cruising down the Ganges to Ceylon, Dhanpati may have tethered his boat to this same banyan tree and cooked his dinner under its shade. To the south is the moss-encrusted paved bathing *ghat*, the stone cracked in many places, eroded in patches. At that ghat is tethered our slim, elegant boat, painted green and white. On its blue flag, inscribed in white lettering, is the name of the boat. Please tell me what the name should be.'

'Should I? Let it be named *Mitali*, for friendship.'

'Just the right name: *Mitali*. I had thought of *Sagari*, in fact I was rather proud of having thought up such a name. But you have defeated me, I must admit. Through the garden flows a narrow channel, bearing the pulsebeat of the Ganges. You live on one side of the channel, and I live just across, on the other side.'

'Would you swim across every evening, and must I await you at my window, with a lighted lamp?'

'I'll swim across in my imagination, crossing a narrow wooden footbridge. Your house is named *Manasi*, the desired one; and you must give a name to my house.'

'*Deepak* – the lamp.'

'Just the right name. Atop my house, I shall place a lamp to suit the name. A red light will burn there on the evenings when we meet, and a blue one on nights of separation. When I return from Kolkata, I shall daily expect a letter from you. It should sometimes reach me, sometimes not. If I don't receive it by eight in the evening, I shall curse my ill-fortune and try to read Bertrand Russell's textbook on logic. It will be our rule, that I must never visit you uninvited.'

'And can I visit you?'

'Ideally, both of us should follow the same rule, but if you occasionally break it, I shall not find it intolerable.'

'If the rule is not to be observed in the breaking, what would be the condition of your house? Perhaps I should visit you in a *burqha*.'

'That's all very well, but I want my letter of invitation. The letter need contain nothing but a few lines of verse, taken from some poem.'

'And will there be no invitations for me? Am I to be discriminated against?'

'You are invited once a month, on the night when the moon is at its full, after fourteen days of fragmented existence.'

'Now offer your favourite pupil an example of the kind of letter to be written.'

'Very well.' He produced a notebook from his pocket and wrote, first in English, then in Bengali:

'Blow gently over my garden
     Wind of the southern sea
In the hour my love cometh
     And calleth me.'

Labanya did not return the piece of paper to him.

'Now for an example of the kind of letter you would write. Let's see how much you have gained from your lessons.'

Labanya was about to write on a piece of paper. 'No,' insisted Amit, 'you must write in this notebook of mine.'

Labanya wrote, in Sanskrit, and then in English:

'Mita, twamasi mama jivanam, twamasi mama
     bhushanam,
     Twamasi mama bhavajaladhiratnam.
Mita, you are my life, my adornment,
     The jewel in the ocean of my world.'

'The amazing thing is, I have written the words of a woman, and you the words of a man,' remarked Amit, putting the notebook in his pocket. 'There is nothing incongruous about it. Whether the wood comes from a red silk cotton tree or from a *bakul* tree, when set alight, the fire looks the same.'

'So, after the invitations, what next?' Labanya wanted to know.

'The evening star has risen,' Amit replied. 'The Ganges is in high tide; a breeze ripples through the rows of fir trees; the waves lap against the roots of the ancient banyan tree. Behind your house is *Padmadighi*, the large pond; there, you bathe at the secluded *ghat* and plait your hair. You wear a different colour each day; as I approach, I wonder what colour you would wear this evening. There is no fixed place for our meeting: sometimes, it's the paved area beneath the champa tree, sometimes the rooftop of your house, sometimes the riverside terrace. I shall bathe in the Ganges, and wear a white muslin *dhoti* and wrap, with ivory-inlaid wooden sandals on my feet. I'll find you reclining on a carpet, waiting for me with a silver platter containing a jasmine garland, a tiny bowl of sandalwood paste, and on the side, some burning incense. During the Durga *Puja*, we'll go on a holiday, the two of us, for at least a couple of months. But we'll go our separate ways. If you go to the hills, I shall head for the seas. Thus I present to you my formula for our conjugal dual rule. Now tell me your opinion.'

'I am willing to follow the formula.'

'There is a difference between following a formula and embracing something with your whole heart, *Banya*.'

'Even if I don't require what is necessary for you, I shall still raise no objections.'

'Have you no requirements?'

'No, none. However close, you would still remain at a great distance from me. It would be pointless for me to preserve that distance by means of any formulae. But I know there is nothing in me which can withstand your close scrutiny without causing me shame; hence I would feel safer if the two of us spent our married life in separate palaces, located on opposite shores.'

'I can't let you win, *Banya*!' exclaimed Amit, rising to his feet. 'Let my garden-estate go. We shall not step outside Kolkata. I shall hire a room on the floor above Niranjan's office, for a rent of seventy-five rupees. There you will live, and so will I. In the heaven of our souls, there is no distinction between distance and proximity. To the left of our five-foot wide bed will be your palace, *Manasi*, and to the right, my *Deepak*. On the eastern wall of the room will be a dresser with a mirror, in which we shall see both our faces reflected. To the west will be our bookshelf, its back blocking the sun, its front housing the only circulating library available to its two readers. To the north of the room will be a sofa; I shall occupy a corner of it on the left, leaving some space. You will stand, concealed by the *alna*, our clothes-rack. Just a couple of feet away, I shall hold up with trembling hands your letter of invitation; it will say:

'Blow gently across the terrace,
O southerly breeze,
For in an instant, my eyes
Will meet my beloved's.

'Does this sound awkward, *Banya*?'

'Not at all, *Mita*. But what is the source?'

'The notebook of my friend Nilmadhav. His future wife's identity was not known for certain at the time these lines were composed. Addressing her, he had recast the English poem in the Kolkata mould, and I had aided his efforts. Having obtained an M.A. in Economics, the man brought home his new bride, complete with a dowry of fifteen thousand rupees and eight *bharis* of gold jewellry. They gazed into each other's eyes, the southerly breeze also blew, but he was unable to make any further use of those lines of verse. Now, his collaborator will not hesitate to lay claim to the complete meaning of that poem.'

'The southerly breeze will blow across your terrace as well, but will your new bride remain forever new?'

'So she will, she will, she will!' proclaimed Amit in a loud voice, thumping the table forcefully.

'What will remain, Amit?' inquired Yogamaya, rushing in from the next room. 'My table, it seems, will not remain much longer.'

'Whatever is durable in this world will remain. A new bride is hard to find in this world, but if by good fortune, one such in a million is discovered, she will remain a new bride forever.'

'Can you offer an example?'

'I shall one day, when the time is ripe.'

'That will take some time, it seems; meanwhile, let's have lunch.'

12
The Final Evening

'I leave for Kolkata tomorrow, *Mashima*,' Amit informed them after lunch. 'My relatives have begun to suspect that I have adopted tribal ways.'

'How would your relatives know that words could bring about such a transformation in you?'

'They know only too well. Else, what are relatives for? But it's not a matter of words, or of taking to tribal ways. Is my transformation merely a change of caste? It's an epochal transition! Between then and now, a whole era has passed, like a *kalpanta* – the four-hundred-and-thirty-two million solar years that make up a day and night in the life of Brahma. Prajapati, god of marriage, has awakened in my heart, in a new form. *Mashima*, please permit me to take Labanya for an outing today. Before my departure, let the two of us offer joint obeisance to the hills of Shillong.'

Yogamaya assented. As they walked, their hands touched, their bodies drew close. From the edge of the secluded path, the deep forests sloped downwards. Somewhere in the forest was a clearing, where a patch of sky, suffused with the fading glow of sunset, could be glimpsed above the watchful mountains. At that spot, the two of them came to a halt and stood, facing west. Drawing Labanya's head to his heart, Amit raised her face. Tears trickled from the corners of her half-closed eyes. Against the golden backdrop of the sky, the light faded in myriad tints, like melting rubies and emeralds. Here and there, through gaps in the clouds, the deep blue of the sky could be seen; it seemed to resonate with the unspoken echoes of that immortal realm where there is no bodily existence, only pure joy. Slowly, the darkness deepened. Like a flower at dusk, the open patch of sky seemed to close its many-hued petals.

'Let's go now,' said Labanya softly, her head resting on his breast. Somehow, at this point, she felt it was best to bring things to an end.

Amit sensed this, but said nothing. He clasped Labanya's head to his chest just once, before they turned back and retraced their steps, very slowly.

'I must set out early tomorrow morning,' he told her. 'I shall not visit you again before I leave.'

'Why not?'

'The Shillong chapter of our story has ended at the right place today. Here endeth the first canto, entitled "Our Very Own Paradise".'

Labanya walked on in silence, hand-in-hand with Amit. There was joy in her heart, and mingled with it, a silent grief. Never again in her life, she felt, would she come so intimately close to grasping the unimaginable. After such an auspicious *shubhodrishti* – the ritual meeting of eyes between bride and groom – was a ceremonial wedding night required? There remained only a last obeisance to be offered, a combined salute to their union and their parting. She felt a strong urge to make that gesture now: to say to Amit, 'You have made me blessed.' But that was not to be.

'*Banya*, say your last words to me in the form of a poem,' requested Amit, 'so I can easily carry them as a memory. Recite to me some lines that you remember.'

Labanya thought for a while, then recited:

'*I did not bring you joy, but gave you freedom,*
My prayer-offering, when daylight dawned.
Nothing else remains: no prayer, nor the poverty
Of each passing moment, no reproachful words,
No petty tears, nor the laughter of arrogance;
No looking back. I only filled my prayer-basket
With the gift of my death, to offer you liberty.'

'*Banya*, that was unfair. Never! Such words are not to be uttered on a day like this. Why did you think of these lines? Please take back this poem of yours immediately.'

'Have no fear, *Mita*. This love, tested by fire, claims no happiness; it liberates because it is free; it does not lead to exhaustion or decline. What more can one offer?'

'But I want to know where you found this poem.'

'It's Robi Thakur's.'

'I have not come across it in any of his books.'

'It has not been published in any book.'

'Then how did you come upon it?'

'There was a young man who respected my father as his guru. My father had fed his appetite for knowledge. The young man, too, was devoted to the pursuit of the sacred. Whenever he had the opportunity, he would approach Robi Thakur and beg for morsels from his notebooks, carrying them back as frugal alms.'

'And he would offer those morsels at your feet.'

'He wouldn't dare. He would leave them around, hoping they would catch my attention, hoping I would pick them up.'

'Did you show him kindness?'

'I did not find the opportunity. I pray in my heart of hearts that the Lord would show him kindness.'

'It is abundantly clear to me, that the poem you recited today actually echoes the private emotions of this unfortunate man.'

'Yes, indeed it does.'

'Then why did you remember this poem today?'

'How can I say? There was another fragment of verse to accompany it; I can't say why that, too, comes to mind on this occasion:

'O beauteous one, you bear the gift
    Of tears that fill your eyes.
Clasped to your bosom, you carry
    The flame of sacrifice.
It brightens sorrow, breaks the magic spell
    That holds the heart enchanted.
In its warmth, our parting blossoms
    Like a hundred-petalled lotus.'

'*Banya*, why has this young man come between us today?' protested Amit, clasping Labanya's hand. 'I'm not jealous, for I detest jealousy. But a strange apprehension troubles my mind. Tell me, why did these poems, his gifts to you, surface in your memory in this fashion, on this very day?'

'The day he bid us farewell and departed from our house, I discovered these two poems on his writing-desk. I found them along with many other unpublished poems by Robi Thakur, almost enough to fill a notebook. Today, it's my turn to bid you farewell. Perhaps that is why I remembered these lines written in parting.'

'Is there no difference between those farewells and this one?'

'How can I tell? But this argument is totally unnecessary. I have simply recited to you the poetry that appeals to me: perhaps that's all there is to it.'

'*Banya*, until people have completely forgotten Robi Thakur's writings, his best work will not really be recognised. That's why I don't quote his poems at all. The appreciation of partisan readers is like a fog that soils the brightness of the sky with its damp touch.'

'Look, *Mita*, women's taste regards the object of adoration as an exclusive personal possession, to be cherished in the private chambers of the heart. It takes no account of public opinion, offering the highest price it can afford, without comparing prices with others to ascertain the object's market-value.'

'Then there is hope for me as well, *Banya*. Concealing the tiny stamp that bears my market-price, I shall proudly sport a large sign stating your estimate of my worth.'

'We are nearing our house, *Mita*. Let me hear you recite the poem that will mark your journey's end.'

'Don't be annoyed *Banya*, but I can't recite lines from Robi Thakur.'

'Why would I be annoyed?'

'I have discovered a writer, whose style…'

'I regularly hear you speak of him. I've ordered his books from Kolkata.'

'What a disaster! His books! The man may have many other faults, but he never tries to publish a book. It is through me that you must gradually get to know him. Or else…'

'Have no fear, *Mita*, I am convinced that I can learn to understand him exactly as you do. Victory shall be mine.'

'How?'

'What I acquire through my own taste is mine, and what I shall gain through your taste will also be mine. I shall reach out with both hands to receive the joint offering of both our hearts. In your tiny room in Kolkata, on a single shelf of your bookcase, I shall be able to accommodate the works of both the poets of our choice. Now recite your poem.'

'I no longer have the inclination. All these intervening arguments have ruined the atmosphere.'

'It's not ruined at all! The atmosphere is fine.'

Flicking back his hair, Amit began to declaim in a highly emotional tone:

'*O beauteous morning star!*
    From beyond the distant mountain-peaks,
Reveal yourself, at night's end,
    To the lost wayfarer.

'Do you understand, *Banya*? The moon beckons the morning star, to be his companion for the night. He is unhappy with the way his own night has turned out.

'*Where earth meets sky, I linger.*
    I am the moon, half-awake,
The cleavage, half in shadow,
    On the bosom of the dark.

108

'This half-awake condition of the moon, his faint, glimmering light, makes only a slight dent in the darkness. That's the cause of his anguish. Caught in this web of shallowness, longing to tear it apart, he seems to have simmered with resentment during his nightlong sleep. What an idea! How grand it sounds!

> '*Deep in slumber, the universe waits,*
> > *For me to ascend my shrine.*
> *In dreams, I strum my instrument,*
> > *To ruffle the surface of its sleep.*

'But then, the burden of such a shallow existence is too much to bear; debris collects in the sluggish flow of a dwindling river; a trivial person finds it fatiguing to carry his own weight. Hence, he says:

> '*With slow steps I head for the shore.*
> > *My journey is done.*
> *My voice falters as I sing,*
> > *My limbs flag in tiredness.*

'But is such fatigue to be the end of him? There is hope that his slack strings will be freshly tuned; for, from beyond the horizon, he seems to hear someone's footsteps:

> '*O beauteous morning star!*
> > *Come swiftly, before night's end.*
> *Complete, in our waking hours,*
> > *The speech that was lost in our dreams.*

'There is hope of salvation, for he can hear the immense commotion of the awakened universe. The harbinger of that great journey is about to appear, bearing a lamp in her hands:

> *'Retrieve the words from the depths of night,*
> > *And offer them to the dawn.*
> *In darkness, speech had lost itself:*
> > *Now, let it shine in glory.*
> *Where torpor disappears,*
> > *Where celestial music is heard,*
> *There, I offer up my veena:*
> > *I, the moon, half-awake.*

'I am that unfortunate moon, of course. Tomorrow, I depart. But I don't want to depart in emptiness. Presiding over the event, the beauteous morning star will arise, chanting the song of awakening. At dawn, the beauteous morning star will bring to completion all that had remained indistinct in the dreams of a life filled with darkness. This poem reveals the power of hope, the shining glory of the morning to come: it's not the wilting, despairing lamentation of your Robi Thakur's verse.'

'Why are you so angry, Mita? Robi Thakur can only accomplish what is within his power, no more: why say the same thing over and over again?'

'All of you give him too much...'

'Don't say that, *Mita*. My taste is mine alone; if my likings coincide with someone else's, or fail to coincide with yours, am I to blame for that? Let me promise, then, that if I ever find a place in that seventy-five-rupee abode of yours, then you may recite to me the verses of your favourite poet, but I shall not recite to you the verses of mine.'

'But that would be unjust. To accept with bowed head the torment inflicted by each partner upon the other – that's what marriage is all about.'

'But you can never tolerate the torment inflicted by taste. At the festival of taste, you don't allow any uninvited guest; but I welcome even a passing stranger.'

'I shouldn't have provoked this argument. It has brought a discordant note into the harmony of this, our last evening here together.'

'Not at all! Our harmony is created from the notes that ring true even after we have spoken our minds plainly. In it, there are no limits to forgiveness.'

'I must subdue the bitter taste in my mouth, today. But not with Bengali verse. English poetry helps me keep my cool, to a great extent. After my return to India, I, too, had done a short stint as a professor.'

'Our intellect is like the English bulldog,' laughed Labanya. 'It barks at the merest sight of swaying *dhoti* pleats, having no conception of the protocol that obtains among *dhoti*-wearers. Instead, it wags its tail upon seeing the badge on a cook's livery.'

'I must admit that's true. A bias is not a natural thing. In most cases, it's created on demand. One has developed a habitual bias for English literature, from regular discipline and chastisement during childhood. On account of that habit, one lacks the courage to condemn one party, or to praise the other. Never mind. There shall be no Nibaran Chakrabarti today, only pure English verse, without translation.'

'No, no, *Mita*, let your English be, leave that for the study table at home. Tonight, our last poem must be one by Nibaran Chakrabarti. No other poet will do.'

'Victory to Nibaran Chakrabarti!' exclaimed Amit, in glee. 'At last, he has become immortal. *Banya*, I shall make him your court poet. He shall seek favours only at your doorstep, nowhere else.'

'Will that always satisfy him?'

'If not, we shall pull his ears and dismiss him.'

'Well, we shall decide about the ear-pulling later. Now recite the poem.'

Amit began to recite:

'How patiently you stayed,
          Day and night, by my side!
How frequently your footprints left their mark
          On my fortune's dusty path!
                    Now, when I must depart
                         For a place far away,
          I shall sing to you
               Of your own victory.
How often, in our lives,
          The fire of sacrifice fails to ignite,
          Spirals of smoke rising
Into empty space with a sigh!
How often, a momentary flame
          Faintly draws a mark
On the brow of darkness insensate,
Only to vanish without trace!
          But now, upon your advent,
               The sacred fire burns

In full glory.
Blessed will be my holy sacrifice.
At the day's end, to you I dedicate
My final prayer-offering.
Accept my homage,
The fruits of my life's endeavour.
Bless me with your tender touch,
As I bow at your feet.
Where you reign in splendour,
Upon your glorious throne,
Summon me to you.
There, let my prayer find a place.'

13
Apprehensions

Next morning, Labanya found it difficult to concentrate on her work. She had even missed her morning walk. Both she and Amit were responsible for ensuring that he kept his vow not to visit her before leaving Shillong. That morning, Amit would have to take the route along which she usually took her daily walk. So, she was sorely tempted, and had to curb her eagerness with great difficulty. Yogamaya would customarily pluck some flowers for her prayers, after an early bath. Before she emerged outdoors, Labanya left that part of the garden to seek out the shade of the eucalyptus tree. She carried a couple of books, perhaps to delude herself as well as others. A book lay open, but the hours passed, and the page was not turned. In her heart was the persistent feeling that her days of celebration were over. From time to time this morning, she felt the harbinger of separation flash his message across the sky, in the gaps between cloud and sunshine. She felt a deep conviction that Amit was an eternal fugitive, never to be found once he had slipped away. During their journey together, he would begin a narrative. Then, night would descend, and the next morning it would be discovered that the wayfarer had vanished, leaving his story incomplete, full of loose ends. So Labanya was sure that his narrative would forever remain unfinished. Today, the gloom of that incompleteness could be felt in the morning light, and the mournful breeze was laden with the weariness of an untimely decline.

Meanwhile, at nine in the morning, Amit burst noisily into the house, calling out, '*Mashima*! *Mashima*!' Morning prayers over, Yogamaya was busy sorting daily provisions. Today, she, too, felt troubled. All these days, Amit had filled her loving heart and home with his garrulity, good humour and liveliness. Weighed down by the sorrow of his departure, her morning drooped like a flower cast down by the weight of falling raindrops. Today, in this household racked with the pain of separation, she had not summoned Labanya to assist her with daily chores, realising that she needed to be alone, away from the public eye.

Labanya jumped to her feet, the book slipping from her lap without her noticing it. Meanwhile, Yogamaya came rushing out of the storeroom.

'What's this, Amit, my boy, is there an earthquake?' she cried.

'An earthquake, indeed. My baggage was dispatched, the car arranged, when I went to the post office to check for mail. There, I found a telegram.'

'All is well, I hope?' enquired Yogamaya anxiously, watching his expression.

Labanya joined them in the room.

'My sister Sissy is arriving this very evening, along with her friend Katy Mitter, and Katy's elder brother Naren,' Amit informed her, with great agitation.

'So what's there to worry about, my son? There's a vacant house beside the racing track, I'm told. If that's unavailable, can't we offer them accommodation of sorts at my place?'

'I have no worry on that score, Mashi. They have booked themselves into a hotel on their own.'

'Under no circumstances can we let your sisters come here to find you living in that godforsaken cottage, son. They will blame us for the madness of their own kinfolk.'

'No, Mashi, mine is a case of paradise lost. I must bid goodbye to that paradise of bare essentials. My dreams of happiness must fly from their nesting place in that rope-strung cot. I, too, must seek refuge in some ultra-civilised room of that ultra-clean hotel.'

The words were not particularly significant, yet Labanya's face grew pale. It had not occurred to her, all these days, that Amit's social world was a thousand leagues removed from her own. In an instant, this realisation dawned on her. Amit's imminent departure for Kolkata had not borne the harsh semblance of separation. But from his compulsion to move into a hotel today, Labanya understood that the home which the two of them had until now been building in their imagination, with various invisible ingredients, would perhaps never materialise.

'Whether I move to a hotel or to hell, this house remains my real home,' declared Amit to Yogamaya, after a brief glance at Labanya.

Amit had realised that the arrival of visitors from the city did not bode well. He was mentally conjuring up many plans to prevent Sissy and her group from visiting this house. But of late, his mail had been directed to Yogamaya's address, for he had not anticipated then that this could one day become a source of trouble. Amit's inner feelings were not readily repressed; rather, he tended to overstate them. His extreme anxiety about his sister's visit had struck Yogamaya as excessive. Labanya, too, felt herself a source of embarrassment for Amit where his sisters were concerned. She found this a distasteful, humiliating thought.

'Do you have time to spare?' Amit asked Labanya. 'Would you care to go out with me?'

'No, I have no time,' was Labanya's rather harsh reply.

'Why, my child, why not go out for a while?' Yogamaya urged her, anxiously.

'Korta Ma, I have really neglected Suroma's studies of late. It was remiss of me. I decided last night that I must not show any slackness today.' With these words, Labanya pursed her lips, her face grim.

Yogamaya was familiar with Labanya's stubbornness. She did not dare pester her.

'I, too, must set out to do my duty,' said Amit, in a listless tone. 'I must see that things are in order for their arrival.'

Before taking his leave, he paused for a moment in the veranda. 'Look, *Banya*,' he urged. 'Beyond the trees, you can catch a brief glimpse of the thatched roof of my cottage. I haven't told you yet, but I have bought that cottage. The owner is surprised. She probably thinks I've discovered a secret gold mine there. She has substantially raised the price of the property. I had indeed discovered a gold mine there, something known only to me. The wealth of my shabby hovel will remain hidden from everyone's eyes.'

Labanya's face was shadowed with a deep sadness. 'Why do you think so much about what everyone would say?' she demanded. 'So what if everyone got to know? Indeed, they ought to know the truth about us, so nobody would dare to show any disrespect.'

'*Banya*, I've decided we must spend a few days in that very cottage, after we are married,' Amit informed her, without answering her directly. 'My garden-estate on the shores of the Ganges, that *ghat* of ours, that banyan tree, they have all merged into that cottage. *Mitali*, the name of your choice, suits that cottage alone.'

'You have left that cottage today, *Mita*. If you try to re-enter it on some other occasion, you will find it too small to accommodate you. In today's home, there is no room for tomorrow. You had said, the other day, that in life a person's first struggle is with poverty, the second with wealth. But you didn't speak of the third phase of the sacred endeavour, which has to do with renunciation.'

'*Banya*, that's your Robi Thakur's idea. He writes: 'today, Shah Jahan has even renounced his Taj Mahal.' It doesn't occur to your poet that we create only to transcend the created object. In the created world, that's what is known as evolution. A strange demon possesses one, commanding one to create. With the act of creation, the demon is exorcised, and the created item also becomes redundant. But this doesn't imply that moving on, leaving things behind, is the ultimate goal. In the world, the immortal saga of Shah Jahan-Mumtaz Mahal continues unabated. They are not mere individuals, after all. That's why the Taj Mahal could never be rendered vacant. As a concise postcard-reply to your celebrated poet's *Taj Mahal*, Nibaran Chakrabarti has written a poem about the bridal chamber:

> '*When the night grows restless*
> *At the sound of dawn's chariot-wheels,*
> *I must leave you, O bridal chamber!*

119

In the world outside, alas,
Separation lurks like a fiendish robber.
  Yet, though he may smash and destroy,
And rip apart our wedding-garlands,
  You remain untouched,
  Always;
Your festive celebrations
  Never silenced or disrupted.
Who says the newlyweds have abandoned you,
  Leaving your bed desolate?
   They have not gone away.
At your call, they return
 As new sojourners, knocking
  At your welcoming door.
  Love is undying, O bridal chamber!
  And you, too, are immortal.

'Robi Thakur only speaks of parting, he can't sing of lovers remaining together. Banya, does the poet say that when we, too, knock on that door, it will not open for us?'

'Please *Mita*, I request you not to invoke the war of the poets today. Do you imagine that I have not realised, from the very first day, that you, yourself, are Nibaran Chakrabarti? But don't immediately begin constructing a poetic monument to our love: at least wait for our love to die.'

Labanya realised that Amit, today, was trying to suppress some inner turmoil by saying all sorts of nonsensical things.

Amit, too, sensed that the battle of the poets, though it had not seemed inappropriate yesterday, had struck a discordant note this morning. All the same, he did not like the idea that Labanya saw this clearly, as well.

'Let me go, then,' he proposed, rather dully. 'I, too, have work to do; at the moment, my task is to conduct a survey of hotels. Meanwhile, it seems that for the unfortunate Nibaran Chakrabarti, the honeymoon is over.'

'Look, *Mita*,' pleaded Labanya, clasping Amit's hand, 'I hope you will always be able to forgive me. If ever the moment of our parting arrives, I beseech you not to abandon me in anger.' She rushed to the adjoining room, to hide her tears.

For a while, Amit stood stock still. Then, slowly and absently, he went to stand beneath the eucalyptus tree. There, he saw some scattered walnut shells. His heart was seized with pain at the sight. The scattered traces we leave behind us in the course of our lives are pathetic in their very triviality. Then he saw a book lying on the grass: it was Robi Thakur's *Balaka*. The back of the book was damp. He thought once of returning the book, but placed it in his pocket instead. He almost left for the hotel, but again, thought the better of it; instead, he reclined beneath the tree. The damp clouds of night had polished the sky sparkling clean. In the breeze, washed free of dust, the picturesque surroundings were clearly visible. The silhouettes of mountains and trees seemed etched against the deep blue sky. The world, seen up close, seemed to directly touch the heart. The day was declining slowly, to the strains of the *ragini* Bhairavi.

Labanya had vowed she would immediately set about her household chores in real earnest, but espying Amit under the tree she could restrain herself no longer. Her heart heaved, her eyes swam with tears.

'What are you thinking, *Mita*?' she asked, coming up to him.

'The very opposite of what I had thought all these days.'

'It's essential for your well-being to turn your mind upside-down and scrutinise it from time to time. So, let's hear what upside-down thoughts are in your mind.'

'All these days, I kept constructing houses for you in my heart, sometimes beside the Ganges, sometimes atop a mountain. Today, in the morning light, my mind casts up the inviting image of a path, stretching across those mountains, shaded by forests. I walk, clutching a long stick topped by a sharp metal blade; strapped to my back is a square bag. You will accompany me. May your name prove true, *Banya*! Your tide, it seems, has swept me from my enclosed chamber, out onto the open path. In the chamber are all kinds of people, but on the path, only the two of us.'

'The garden-estate at Diamond Harbour was already lost, and now the poor seventy-five-rupee room is gone, as well. Never mind! Let them go. But on our journey, how will you ensure our separation? At the end of the day, will you enter one travellers' inn, and I another?'

'There is no need for that, Banya. The journey makes us new, at every step; there is no time for staleness. Ageing occurs when we remain static.'

'How did this suddenly occur to you, Mita?'

'Very well, let me tell you. I have suddenly received a letter from Shobhanlal. You may have heard of him: he's an expert on the Raichands and Premchands of this world. For some time, he has been out on a journey to discover the ancient travel-routes of Indian history. He wants to retrieve the lost pathways of the past. I want to create pathways for the future.'

Labanya's heart gave a sudden, violent lurch. 'I took the M.A. examination with Shobhanlal, in the same year,' she interrupted. 'I would like to hear all his news.'

'He had once been excited at the prospect of rediscovering the old route through the ancient Afghan city of Kapish. That was the route of Huen Tsang's pilgrimage to India, and before that, of Alexander's military invasion. He earnestly studied Pushto, and practised Pathan customs. With his handsome appearance, dressed in loose-fitting clothes, he didn't look quite like a Pathan, more like a Persian. He came and begged me for a letter of introduction addressed to the French experts who were working in the same field. Some of them had tutored me when I was in France. I gave him the letter, but he was denied permission by Indian government. Ever since then, he wanders in search of old routes in the Himalayas, sometimes in Kashmir, sometimes in Kumaon. Now, he feels the urge to explore the eastern sector of the Himalayas as well. He wants to discover the routes through which Buddhism spread in this region. The thought of that compulsive wanderer makes me melancholy, too. Our sight grows dim scanning the books to find our direction in life, but that lunatic has set out to scan the book of the road, written in the Lord's very own script. Do you know what I think?'

'Tell me.'

'In the first flush of youth, Shobhanlal must have received a blow from some bangle-adorned hand, which flung him from his home onto the streets. I am not clearly acquainted with his whole story, but once when the two of us were alone together, we stayed up chatting till the small hours. Suddenly, from our window, we saw the moon appear behind a flowering jarul tree; at that moment, he tried to tell me about someone. He took no names, nor did he describe her at all; he had barely given me the slightest hint when his voice choked, and he quickly left the room. I could tell that, lodged somewhere in his heart, remains the sting of some extremely cruel experience. That's what he probably tries to erode, step by step, as he travels on his journey.'

Labanya suddenly developed a fascination for botany. She bent low, gazing at a wild flower, yellow and white, blossoming in the grass. She felt a sudden, urgent need to count the petals of the flower, with single-minded concentration.

'Do you know, *Banya*, you have flung me out into the road, today?' Amit asked her.

'How?'

'I had constructed a house. This morning, your words made me feel that you were hesitant to step inside. I have spent two months mentally decorating that house. I called out to you, saying, "Come, my bride, enter my home!" Today, you discarded your bridal finery, and said, "There is no room for us here, my friend. We shall spend our lives walking round the fire."'

The botanical study of wild flowers would not do anymore. Rising to her feet, Labanya pleaded, in anguish, 'Mita! Please say no more! Time is up.'

14
Comet

It took a long time for Amit to realise that his relationship with Labanya was known to all the Bengalis of Shillong. Discussion among clerks in government offices usually centred upon the determination of their own career prospects by the position of ruling planets on their professional horizon. Then, in the astral sphere of human life, they saw a pair of twin stars appear, emitting light of the first magnitude. The star-gazers, as is their wont, propounded many theories about the fiery drama behind the birth of these two new stars.

Having come to Shillong to savour the mountain air, Kumar Mukherjee, the attorney, had found himself drawn into these theoretical speculations. Some called him Kumar Mukho for short, while others nicknamed him Mar Mukho, the One on the Warpath! Though not a member of Sissy's private circle, he could be described as her acquaintance, for he belonged to the group of people she knew. Amit had named him Comet Mukho, for, though he did not belong to the coterie, Mukho would occasionally sweep his tail across their orbit. It was everybody's guess that he was especially attracted by the planet named Lissy. This was a source of general amusement, but Lissy herself was annoyed and embarrassed about it. Hence, she would often vigorously wrench his tail in passing, but clearly, this made no difference to the comet, for his head and tail remained intact.

Amit had caught an occasional distant glimpse of Kumar Mukho on the streets of Shillong. It would be hard

125

not to spot him. Because he had not yet been to England, Mukho's English style was flagrantly visible. Between his lips would be a thick, heavy cigar, the main reason for the nickname Comet. Amit tried to avoid him by keeping a safe distance, deluding himself that the Comet had not sensed this. But to see without taking any notice takes immense skill, just like the art of burglary. The proof of its success lies in evading detection. It requires expertise in fixing one's gaze somewhere far beyond the scene before one's eyes.

From the Bengali social circles of Shillong, Kumar Mukho had culled many facts which could be broadly classified under the heading: 'The Excesses of Amit Raye'. The persons most vocal in their criticism had secretly derived the greatest relish from the situation. Kumar had planned to spend some time in Shillong to mend a disorder in his liver, but his acute urge for rumour-mongering made him hasten back to Kolkata within five days. Once there, by means of his cigar-smoke-filled exaggerations about Amit, he generated a crisis in the Sissy-Lissy circle, arousing a mixture of mockery and inquisitiveness.

The seasoned reader would have guessed by now that Katy Mitter's elder brother Naren was the *vahana*, the sacred beast, devoted to the service of goddess Sissy. There was a rumour that his prolonged devotion would now culminate in marriage. In her heart of hearts, Sissy was amenable to the idea. But by pretending indifference, she had created a haze of uncertainty. Naren had decided to overcome this obstacle by obtaining Amit's consent, but Amit, the humbug, would neither return to Kolkata, nor answer his letters. Like arrows piercing the sound barrier, he had already dispatched in Amit's direction all the English expletives at his command, both in public and in private speech. In fact, he had not baulked at sending an extremely rude telegram to Shillong; but like a firework missile aimed at an indifferent planet, it vanished without leaving any burn-marks. Ultimately, by general consensus, it was decided that the situation demanded an on-the-spot investigation. In the flood-tide of disaster, if they could but catch the slightest glimpse of Amit's floating head, it was their urgent duty to grab him by the forelock and drag him to the safety of the shore. In this respect, the enthusiasm of Amit's own sister Sissy was far exceeded by that of Katy, sister to someone else. Katy Mitter's attitude closely resembled our own political heartburn at the loss of Indian riches to foreign powers.

Naren Mitter had spent a long time in Europe. Son of a *zamindar*, he did not have to worry about earning or spending; his urge for learning was proportionately muted. While abroad, he had concentrated mainly on wasting both time and money. One can simultaneously attain freedom from responsibility and undeserved self-esteem by calling oneself an artist. Therefore, he had inhabited the bohemian quarters of various big cities of Europe, in pursuit of the goddess of art. After some initial attempts, he was forced to give up painting upon the insistence of his plain-spoken well-wishers. Now, he introduced himself as an art critic, for that required no credentials. He could not make art blossom, but was able to mangle it with gusto. In the Parsian mode, he had lovingly sharpened the pointed ends of his moustache, while remaining carefully careless about his unruly head of hair. His appearance was quite pleasant; but in the holy endeavour to improve it further, his dressing table was weighed down with various Parisian forms of self-indulgence. The paraphernalia arranged beside his wash-basin would be excessive even for the ten-headed Ravana's toilet. There was no doubting his noble birth, from the easy nonchalance with which he discarded his expensive Havana cigar after a couple of puffs, to his regular practice of sending his garments by parcel-post to Parisian laundry houses. The best European tailoring-houses kept a record of his measurements in their registers, where one might encounter the aristocratic names of Patiala and Karpurtala. His slang-ridden enunciation of the English tongue was slurred, drawling, and understated, accompanied by the lazy glance of his half-shut eyes; those in the know opined that such inarticulate intensity was to be found in the voices of many rich, blue-blooded Englishmen. In addition, Naren was a role model among his peers for his command of bad language in the form of racecourse swear-words and English oaths.

Katy Mitter's real name was Ketaki. Her deportment was refined, thrice-distilled in her own elder brother's etiquette factory; it contained the pungent essence of British aristocracy. She had arrogantly scissored the ordinary Bengali woman's pride in her long tresses, shedding her hair-knot like a tadpole's tail, with the new convert's eagerness to imitate. The natural fairness of her countenance was enamelled with layers of paint. In the early stages of her life, Katy's dark eyes bore a gentle expression; now, it appeared, she couldn't even see ordinary people. If she did see them, she failed to notice them, and if she did notice them, her glance had the edge of a knife half-unsheathed. In childhood, her lips had a simple sweetness, but now, from frequent sneering, they had developed a permanent resemblance to a hooked elephant-goad. I am inexperienced at describing women's dress. I don't have the vocabulary. To put it in simply, one noticed her wearing a flimsy outer layer, like cast-off snakeskin, through which was visible a hint of inner garments of some other hue. Much of her bosom was exposed; and she made a careful attempt to arrange her bare arms carelessly, now on the table, now on the arms of a chair, now entwined with each other. And when she smoked a cigarette, holding it between two fingers embellished with well-polished nails, it was more for decorative effect than from a desire to inhale the smoke. Most disturbing of all were the intricate postures of her high-heeled shoes. When the Creator forgot that the human foot should be modelled on the goat-hoof, this evolutionary flaw was rectified by the cobbler's gift, the high-heeled shoe, that bizarre device for tormenting the earth with the distorted gait of artificially elevated feet.

Sissy was still at an in-between stage. She had not yet attained the highest degree, but was steadily earning double promotions. In her peals of laughter, excessive cheerfulness and nonstop chatter, there was a constant, bubbling vivacity, highly prized by her admirers. In literary accounts of the adolescent Radha, her manner seems sometimes mature, sometimes naive; this was true of Sissy, as well. Her high-heeled shoes were the victory-gate signalling entry into the new era, but in her knot of uncut hair remained traces of the old order. The lower edge of her sari was draped a few inches too high, but in their extent of exposure, her upper garments still conformed to the bounds of modesty. She wore gloves habitually, for no particular reason, yet she still sported *balas* – thick bangles – on both wrists instead of one. Smoking a cigarette no longer made her dizzy, but she still had a strong addiction to chewing *paan* – betel leaf. She didn't mind having pickles and mango *papad* sent to her, camouflaged in biscuit tins; given the choice between Christmas plum pudding and the *pitha* served at the Poush-festival, she had a slight preference for the latter. Though trained by a white dancer, she demurred at ballroom dancing.

They had rushed to Shillong, all of them, because the wild rumours about Amit had made them anxious. The point of contention was that, according to their definition of class difference, Labanya was a governess, specially created to destroy the caste purity of the men of their own class. They were convinced that it was out of greed for money and prestige that she had clung to Amit so tenaciously. To rescue him from her clutches, it was necessary for the ladies to intervene with their purifying touch. Brahma, the four-faced deity, must have simultaneously glanced at and sided with women with his four pairs of eyes; hence, he had created men to be complete idiots where women were concerned. That explained why, unless assisted by women of their own social group, untouched by class ambitions, men found it so hard to escape the webs of enchantment woven by women of a different class.

At present, the two women had agreed upon the procedure to be adopted for this rescue operation. It was decided that Amit must be kept in the dark at first. The enemy and the battle terrain must first be inspected. Then they could challenge the powers of the sorceress.

The first thing they noticed upon arrival was that Amit had acquired a strong vein of provincialism. Formerly, too, Amit's attitude had not matched that of his coterie. But still, he was then a keen urbanite: scrubbed, polished, shining. Now, it wasn't as if his complexion had darkened from exposure to the open air; rather, it was as if trees and vines had cast their shade upon him. He seemed to have become raw, and in their opinion, somewhat stupid. His deportment was almost like that of ordinary folk. Formerly, he would treat all subjects with an element of humour, but now he had virtually lost that urge. They took this for the ultimate danger signal.

'We had imagined from afar that you were descending into a tribal lifestyle,' Sissy told him bluntly, on one occasion. 'But now we realise that you are ascending into a state of greenness, like the pine trees of this region: healthier, perhaps, than before, but not as interesting.'

Borrowing Wordsworth's idea, Amit retorted that living in close proximity to nature, one's body, mind and soul acquire the stamp of 'mute insensate things'.

We have no complaint against mute, insensate things, thought Sissy to herself; we are concerned about those ultra-sensate beings who specialise in fluent sweet-talk.

They had hoped that Amit himself would bring up the subject of Labanya. A day passed, two days, then three, but he was utterly silent on the subject. Only one thing seemed certain: like a wave-tossed boat, Amit's desires were in turmoil. Even before they were up and dressed, Amit would be back from an outing somewhere; his face then would seem ravaged, like banana leaves shredded by the stormy breeze. Even more disturbing was the fact that some people had spotted a copy of Robi Thakur's works on Amit's bed. On the inside leaf, the first syllable of Labanya's name had been crossed out in red ink. Her name was the touchstone that had probably raised the book's value.

Amit would go out every now and then. 'I'm going to appease my hunger,' he would say. The others were not unaware of the source of the hunger, or of the fact that his hunger was acute. But they would feign ignorance, as if it was impossible to imagine that Shillong could offer anything beyond its air, which increased the appetite. Sissy would smile to herself, while Katy would nurse the burning jealousy in her heart. Amit's own problems loomed so large, that he lacked the power to notice any outward signs of trouble. Hence, he would unabashedly say to his female companions: 'I'm setting out in search of a waterfall.' But he failed to realise that others may have some doubts about the nature of the waterfall and the direction of its flow. This morning, he departed claiming he was going to trade orange honey. Meekly, in very simple language, the two ladies expressed a desire to accompany him, as they felt an irrepressible curiosity about this exquisite honey. The route was difficult, Amit informed them, and could not be negotiated by car. Nipping the discussion in the bud, he rushed away. Noting the restlessness of this bee, the two friends decided to delay no further. It had become imperative to make an expedition to the orchard where the oranges grew. Meanwhile, Naren was at the races. He had been very keen to take Sissy with him, but she did not join him. Who but a sympathetic soul would understand how much self-control such abstinence had entailed?

15
Complications

Having crossed the gate into Yogamaya's garden, the two friends could not spot any servants. Entering the porch, they noticed a teacher and her pupil, studying at a small table on the verandah. It was clear to them that the elder of the two was Labanya.

'I'm sorry,' said Katy, high heels clicking as she stepped onto the verandah.

'Who would you like to meet?' asked Labanya, rising to her feet.

'I came to inquire whether Mister Amit Raye is here,' replied Katy, sweeping Labanya with a sharp glance that took in her entire appearance, from head to toe.

At first, Labanya could not figure out what sort of creature 'Amitraye' might be. 'We don't know him,' she answered.

The two friends exchanged a lightning glance, suppressing a secret smile.

'We are aware that he visits this house more often than is good for him,' Katy flashed back, with a toss of her head.

Startled by her manner, Labanya realised who they were, and what a blunder she had made.

'Let me call Korta Ma, she'll give you news of Amit,' she suggested, flustered.

'Is she your teacher?' Katy inquired curtly of Suroma as soon as Labanya was out of sight.

'Yes.'

'Is Labanya her name?'

'Yes.'

'Got matches?' Katy asked, in English.

Unable to understand this sudden need for matches, Suroma gaped at Katy, mystified.

'Deshlai – matches,' explained Katy.

Suroma fetched a matchbox. Katy lit her cigarette. 'Do you study English?' she asked Suroma, between puffs of smoke.

Suroma nodded in affirmation and immediately rushed from the room.

'Whatever else the girl may have learned from her governess, she certainly hasn't acquired any manners,' remarked Katy.

There followed a discussion between the two friends, much of it in English. 'So this is the famous Labanya! Isn't she delicious! She has turned Shillong into a volcano, splitting Amit's heart, like an earthquake. Silly! Men are funny!'

Sissy laughed out loud. There was generosity in this laughter, for the stupidity of men had not given Sissy cause for complaint. After all, she had created an earthquake even on stony soil, splitting it right apart. But what an unheard-of situation! With a woman like Katy pitted against that strangely dressed governess, a wet blanket, looking as if butter wouldn't melt in her mouth. In her company, the mind would grow mouldy, like a biscuit in rainy weather. How could Amit stand her for a single moment?

'Sissy, your brother's heart has always been topsy-turvy. He has taken a sudden, perverse fancy to this woman, convinced that she is an angel.'

With these words, Katy rested her cigarette against the algebra book on the table, and, taking out her silver-handled cosmetic bag, powdered her nose and darkened her eyebrows with the pencil liner. Sissy was not unduly annoyed by her elder brother's lack of propriety; in fact, she secretly felt rather fond of him. All her anger was directed at the false angels who bask in the admiring gaze of men. Katy lost patience at Sissy's amused indifference about her elder brother. She felt like giving Sissy a hard shake.

At this juncture, Yogamaya appeared on the scene, dressed in white spun silk. Labanya was not with her. Accompanying Katy was a tiny dog named Tabby, his eyes virtually hidden behind his shaggy head of hair. He had sniffed at Labanya and Suroma by way of making acquaintance. Seeing Yogamaya, the dog seemed suddenly excited. Rushing up to her in a show of false affection, he raised his forelegs, his soiled paws leaving their scratchy signature on her pure sari. Sissy caught him by the scruff of his neck and dragged him to Katy. 'Naughty dog!' admonished Katy, wagging a finger in front of his nose.

Katy did not leave her chair. Puffing on her cigarette with an air of detachment, she tilted her head slightly to inspect Yogamaya with a sidelong glance. She was perhaps even more resentful of Yogamaya than of Labanya. She believed that there was a flaw in the official version of Labanya's history. Yogamaya herself, disguised as an aunt, must have tried to trick Amit into marrying the girl. It wouldn't take much intelligence to deceive a man, for the Creator had personally fashioned blinkers for men's eyes.

'I am Ami's sister Sissy,' said Sissy, coming forward and making a faint gesture of greeting.

'Ami calls me *Mashi*, which makes me your *mashi*, too, my child,' responded Yogamaya with a smile.

Observing Katy's attitude, Yogamaya took no notice of her. 'Come, my child, come inside,' she urged Sissy.

'We have no time. We have simply come to ask whether Ami has come here or not,' replied Sissy.

'He's not here yet,' Yogamaya informed her.

'Do you know when he is expected?'

'I can't say for sure. Well, let me find out.'

'The governess who was conducting lessons here pretended she had never met Amit at all!' Katy interrupted sharply, from her chair.

Yogamaya was confused. She realised there must be a problem somewhere. She also understood that it would be difficult to maintain her dignity with these people. Instantly discarding her aunt-like attitude, she retorted, 'I'm told Amitbabu lives in your own hotel, so you should know his whereabouts.'

Katy gave a menacing laugh. 'You may try to hide, but you can't escape,' her laugh implied.

Truth be told, Katy was in a foul temper right from the start, when she first set her eyes on Labanya and was told that the latter didn't know Ami. But Sissy felt only apprehension, no heartburn; she felt drawn to the profundity of Yogamaya's beautiful countenance. She was therefore embarrassed by Katy's deliberate insolence in not rising from her chair to greet Yogamaya. Yet she never dared cross Katy in any matter, for Katy was expert at quelling sedition: she wouldn't tolerate the slightest resistance. She had no qualms about being nasty. Most people are cowardly; when confronted with blatant nastiness, they admit defeat. Katy took a certain pride in her own extreme harshness. She would harass any of her friends who showed signs of what she called 'sweet naïveté'. She boasted of her own rudeness, which she took for forthrightness; those who cringed at such aggressive behaviour felt relieved if they could somehow keep Katy pacified. Sissy belonged to this category. The more she secretly feared Katy, the more she imitated her ways, to demonstrate that she herself was not weak. She didn't always succeed. Katy had realised, today, that in a corner of her mind, Sissy nursed a secret objection to her behaviour. She had therefore deemed it necessary to forcefully demolish Sissy's resistance, before Yogamaya's eyes. She rose to her feet, and placing a cigarette in Sissy's mouth, offered to ignite it with the lighted cigarette in her own mouth. Sissy did not dare refuse. The tips of her ears turned slightly red. All the same, she forced herself to adopt a dismissive air, as if she would snap her fingers at those who frowned upon their modern, westernised habits: as for their disapproval, she cared 'that much for it!'

Exactly at that moment, Amit arrived on the scene. The women were taken aback. He had left the hotel dressed in a felt hat and a British shirt. Now, he was wearing a dhoti and shawl. The scene of his transformation was that very same cottage of his. There, he kept a bookshelf, a wardrobe, and an armchair donated by Yogamaya. After lunch at the hotel he would take refuge in this place. Of late, Labanya had enforced strict discipline; during her lessons with Suroma, nobody was allowed to intrude in search of waterfalls and oranges. Hence, before teatime at half-past four in the evening, Amit was denied permission to visit the house to quench his physical or psychological thirst. He would somehow pass the intervening hours, then dress to pay his visit at the appointed hour.

Today, before he left the hotel, the ring had arrived from Kolkata. He had already imagined himself ceremonially placing the ring on Labanya's finger. Today was special. It would not do to keep this day waiting at the threshold. Today, all work must come to a standstill. He had secretly decided to approach Labanya where she was conducting her lessons, to declare: 'One day, the Emperor arrived on an elephant, but the gate was too low. He turned back, lest he be forced to bow his head. This day, for us, is a great occasion, but you have kept the gates of opportunity too low. Break them down, so the Emperor may enter your home with his head held high.'

Amit also meant to point out that punctuality means arriving at the right moment. But the clock cannot determine the right moment, for it merely knows time by numbers, not the value of time.

Glancing outside, Amit saw that the sky was cloudy, its dimness suggesting that the hour might be five or six in the evening. Like a mother afraid to use the thermometer to check her long-ailing child's temperature once his body feels cool to the touch, Amit avoided looking at his watch, lest its rude message contradict the sky. Today, Amit arrived much earlier than the appointed time. For desperate longing knows no shame.

From the road, one could see the corner of the veranda where Labanya conducted her lessons. Today, he found that spot vacant. His heart leapt for joy. At last, he looked at his watch. It was only twenty minutes past three. The other day, he had said to Labanya that rules are for men to obey, and for the gods to violate; we struggle to observe the law on earth, only to savour the nectar of lawlessness in heaven. Such a heaven sometimes appears on earth. When that happens, one must salute its arrival by breaking all laws. He hoped Labanya would understand the glory of breaking the law; perhaps her heart had felt the touch of a special day, breaking down the fences of everyday routine.

Coming close, he found Yogamaya outside her room, looking on in stupefaction as Sissy lit the cigarette in her mouth from the cigarette in Katy's. He was left in no doubt that the insult was deliberate. Tabby, the dog, rebuffed in his maiden attempt at friendship, was trying to go to sleep at Katy's feet. At Amit's approach, he again grew restive at the prospect of greeting him. Sissy again applied discipline to make him understand that such expressions of goodwill were not welcome in this place.

'*Mashi*!' Amit called out from a distance, and prostrated himself at Yogamaya's feet, without so much as glancing at the two female friends. It was not his custom to touch her feet in this manner. '*Mashima*, where is Labanya?' he demanded.

'How would I know, my child? She's somewhere in the house.'

'But it's not yet time for her lessons to have ended.'

'Upon the arrival of these people, she has probably taken leave and retired to her room.'

'Come, let's go and see what she's doing.' Amit dragged Yogmaya indoors. He completely disregarded the presence at the scene of any other form of life.

'This is an insult! Come, Katy, let's go home!' cried Sissy, rather loudly.

Katy was no less incensed. But she didn't want to leave without witnessing the end.

'It's no use,' argued Sissy.

Katy's enormous eyes were dilated. 'A conclusion must be reached,' she insisted.

Some more time elapsed. 'Let's go, my friend,' repeated Sissy. 'I don't feel like staying a moment longer.'

Katy firmly ensconced herself on the verandah. 'He must depart by this route,' she declared.

Ultimately, Amit emerged, accompanied by Labanya. Her face bore an air of tranquil detachment. There was not the slightest hint of anger, arrogance or reproach. Yogamaya was in the room nearby, but she had no wish to step outside. Amit dragged her out. In an instant, the ring on Labanya's finger caught Katy's eye. The blood rushed to her head, her eyes became bloodshot; she wanted to aim a kick at the whole world.

'*Mashi*, this is my sister Shamita,' Amit said by way of introduction. 'Baba had probably given her a name to rhyme with mine, but there remains the extra syllable. This is my sister's friend Ketaki.'

Meanwhile, there was another disturbance. When Suroma's cat emerged from the room, Tabby's canine logic saw this act of daring as a legitimate reason for declaring war. He would advance from time to time to bark at her, but upon encountering the hissing cat with its claws unsheathed, would retreat again in some doubt about the possible outcome of the battle. In this predicament, deciding that growling mildly from afar was the only safe way of demonstrating his heroism, he began to make an incessant noise. Without responding in any way, the cat arched its back and left the scene. Katy could bear it no more. She pulled the dog's ears with intense rage. Much of this ear-pulling was directed at her own ill fortune. The dog squealed in shrill protest against such maltreatment. Fortune smiled, in silent amusement.

When the commotion had subsided, Amit addressed his sister: 'Sissy, this is Labanya. You have not heard me mention this name, but you must have heard of it from sundry other people. Our wedding has been fixed for the month of Agrahayan, in Kolkata.'

Katy wasted no time in summoning up a smile. 'I congratulate you,' she declared. 'The orange-honey wasn't hard to access, it appears. The quest was not difficult, for the honey had leapt forth to offer itself to your lips, of its own accord.'

Sissy burst into her customary giggle.

Labanya realised that this was a barbed comment, but could not fathom its full meaning.

'When I set forth this morning, they asked me where I was going,' Amit explained to her. 'I told them I was going in search of honey. That's why they are amused. It's my fault, actually; people can't tell when I'm not being facetious.'

'Victory is yours, as far as orange-honey goes,' intervened Katy, calmly enough. 'Now make sure that I don't lose out, either.'

'Tell me what I must do.'

'I have a wager with Naren. He had insisted you would never go to the races, because nobody could persuade you to visit a place frequented by gentlemen. I had wagered this diamond ring on taking you to the races with me. I combed the waterfalls and honey-shops of this area, until I finally ran you to earth here. Sissy, why don't you tell him what a "wild goose chase" this has been, if I may borrow an expression from the English?'

Sissy smiled wordlessly.

'Do you remember that story, Amit, the one you told me yourself?' pursued Katy. 'Some Persian philosopher, unable to trace the thief who stole his turban, had ultimately chosen to wait for the culprit at the graveyard. From here, there could be no escape, he had argued. I was temporarily thrown off the scent when Miss Labanya said she didn't know him, but my heart assured me that, sooner or later, he would have to reach this place, his own graveyard.'

Sissy laughed out loud.

'Amit didn't utter your name,' Katy informed Labanya. 'He used honeyed terms to describe you as orange-honey, while you, being too simple to speak in riddles, blurted out that you didn't know Amit at all. Yet, there was no retribution for you in the Sunday-school mode: fate, the divine arbiter, imposed no penalty on the two of you. One of you consumed the hard-won honey in a single gulp, and the other grew familiar with a stranger at a single glance. Now, must I, alone, be condemned to suffer defeat? Sissy, just imagine how unjust this would be!'

Another shrill laugh from Sissy. Tabby the dog, deeming it his social duty to join in this exuberance, showed signs of excitement. For the third time, he had to be restrained.

'You know, Amit, that if I lost this diamond ring, nothing in the world would console me,' pleaded Katy. 'This ring was once your gift to me. It has never left my finger for a moment; it has become part of my body. Must I ultimately part from it here, in the mountains of Shillong, by losing a wager?'

'Why did you have to place a wager, my friend?' inquired Sissy.

'From my secret pride in myself, and faith in other human beings. My pride has been demolished; the race is over, and this time, I stand defeated. I can't persuade Amit anymore, it seems. Well, if you must inflict this strange form of defeat on me, then why did you give me this ring with so much affection? Did that gift not signify any commitment? Didn't it imply a pledge to protect me from humiliation?'

As she spoke, Katy's voice became choked with emotion. She held back her tears with difficulty.

Seven years ago, when Katy was eighteen, Amit had removed the ring from his finger and transferred it to hers. They were both in England at the time. At Oxford, there was a young man infatuated with Katy. On that day, Amit had defeated this Punjabi youth in a friendly rowing competition. In the June moonlight, the sky seemed to speak out loud; the profusion of flowers blossoming in the meadows made the earth restless. At such a moment, Amit had placed his ring on Katy's finger. In his heart

145

were many thoughts, unexpressed; but nothing remained concealed. At that time, Katy's face had not acquired its coat of make-up; her smile was artless, and her countenance did not try to hide its blush in the heat of emotion. Once the ring was on her finger, Amit had whispered to her:

'Tender is the night
And haply the queen moon is on her throne.'

Katy was not yet skilled in the art of conversation. She had simply sighed, as if saying to herself, '*Mon ami*,' the French expression for 'My intimate friend'.

On this present occasion, Amit, too, found himself at a loss for words. He could think of nothing to say.

'If I have lost the wager, then let this permanent token of my defeat remain with you, Amit. I shall not let it sustain a falsehood by keeping it on my finger.'

With these words, Katy removed the ring from her finger, placed it on the table, and hurried away. Tears flowed profusely down her enamelled cheeks.

16
Liberation

Labanya received a brief note from Shobhanlal:

> *I arrived in Shillong last night. If you grant permission, I shall visit you. If not, I depart tomorrow. You have punished me, but to this day, I have not clearly understood when and how I have given you offence. I come to beg you for an explanation; otherwise, I shall have no peace of mind. Have no fear. I have nothing else to ask of you.*

Labanya's eyes filled with tears. She wiped them away. In silence, she reviewed her own past. She recalled the pathetic timidity of the tender seedling of love, which could have blossomed, had she not stifled it and prevented its growth. She could have cherished the seedling and brought it to fruition by now. But at that time, she had been proud of her learning, devoted single-mindedly to the pursuit of knowledge, full of arrogant independence. Observing her father's fascination for learning, she had mentally condemned love as a form of weakness. Today, love had avenged itself, and her pride was forced to bite the dust. What would then have been as easy as breathing or simple laughter now seemed extremely difficult. Today, she hesitated to welcome with open arms this person who had once been a passing visitor in her life; yet her heart broke at the thought of relinquishing him. She remembered Shobhanlal in his moment of humiliation, the inarticulate anguish on his face. Such a long time had elapsed since then! What nectar had sustained that unrequited love in this young man's heart? It must have been the inner nobility of his own nature.

Labanya wrote:

You are my greatest friend. I do not, now, possess the wealth to repay you adequately for this friendship. You have never demanded a price; this time, too, you offer all you have to give, claiming nothing in return. I have neither the power nor the arrogance to spurn your gift with feigned indifference.

She had dispatched the letter when Amit came to her and proposed: '*Banya*, let's go out today, the two of us.'

Amit had made the suggestion rather timidly, fearing that Labanya might now refuse to accompany him.

'Let's go,' agreed Labanya, quite readily.

They set out together, the two of them. With some hesitation, Amit tried taking Labanya's hand in his. Without the slightest hint of resistance, Labanya let him hold her hand. Amit pressed her hand hard, unable to communicate in words anything beyond the emotions this pressure might convey. They walked up to the same clearing in the forest which they had visited the other day. Touching a treeless mountain top with its declining rays, the sun disappeared from view. The exquisite greenish glow slowly faded to a deep, tender blue. The two of them stopped to gaze in that direction.

'Why did you use me to remove the ring you had once placed on someone else's finger?' asked Labanya, very softly.

'How can I explain everything to you, Banya?' protested Amit, stung by her words. 'The person to whom I had once presented the ring, and the person who today removed it from her finger, are they one and the same?'

'One was the product of the Creator's love, the other of your negligence,' Labanya declared.

'That's not entirely true,' argued Amit. 'I alone am not responsible for the suffering that has produced the Katy we see today.'

'But Mita, when a person had completely surrendered herself to you, why didn't you cherish her as your own? For some reason, you slackened your grip on her before she felt the pressure of sundry other grasping hands, transforming her very image. It's because she lost your love one day that she set about decorating herself in ways that would appeal to others. Today, she appears to me like a doll in an English toy shop; this could never have happened had her heart remained alive. But let such things be. I have one request to make. You must keep it.'

'Sure, just tell me what it is.'

'Take your companions to Cherrapunji on a holiday, for at least a week. You can entertain her, even if you can't bring her happiness.'

'Very well,' agreed Amit, after a short silence.

'Let me tell you something, Mita,' said Labanya, resting her head against his breast. 'I'll never bring up the matter again. You don't bear the slightest responsibility for the inner bond that exists between us. I don't say this in anger; I insist with all my love that you should not offer me your ring, for there is no need for tokens between us.

Let my love be immaculate, bearing no mark, no shadow, of the external world.'

With these words, she removed the ring from her finger and slowly placed it on his. Amit did not stop her.

Quietly, glowing with tranquility, Labanya lifted her countenance towards Amit's, like the earth, at dusk, silently raising its face to a sky suffused with the glow of the setting sun.

As soon as a week had elapsed, Amit returned to Yogamaya's house. The house was locked, everyone was gone. They had left no forwarding address.

Amit stood beneath the same eucalyptus tree, then wandered about for a while, with an empty heart.

The gardener, a familiar face, came up and inquired: 'Should I unlock the house? Would you like to wait inside?'

'Yes,' replied Amit, after some hesitation.

Entering the house, he went into Labanya's sitting room. The chairs, tables, shelves were still there, but the books were gone. Scattered on the floor were a few torn, empty envelopes, bearing Labanya's name and address, inscribed in an unfamiliar hand; on the table, a few used and dis- carded pen nibs, and a used-up, tiny pencil stub. He put the pencil in his pocket. In the bedroom immediately adja- cent, there was only a mattress on the iron bedstead, and on the dressing table, an empty bottle of oil. Resting his head on his arms, Amit lay down on the mattress, making the bed creak. There was a dumb emptiness about the room. It could answer no questions. It had collapsed into a fainting fit from which it would never again awaken.

Afterwards, Amit returned to his own cottage, a heavy lassitude weighing down his heart and body. Everything was exactly as he had left it. In fact, Yogamaya had not even reclaimed her armchair. He realised that she had left him this chair out of affection; he seemed to hear her quiet, tender voice calling to him – 'My boy!' In a gesture of obeisance, Amit prostrated himself before that chair.

The mountains of Shillong had lost all their charm. He could find no solace anywhere.

17
Parting lines

Jatishankar was a student at Kolkata University. He stayed at the Kalutola Mess in Presidency College. Amit would often invite him home for a meal, read all sorts of books with him, startle him with all kinds of strange conversation, or take him for a drive.

After that, Jatishankar lost touch with Amit for a while, and had no definite news of his whereabouts. Sometimes he would hear that Amit was in Nainital, sometimes in Utakamand. One day, he heard a common friend say jokingly that Amit was now striving to alter Katy Mitter's outer complexion. He had found a task after his own heart: to transform the very colour of a person's identity. All these days, Amit had depended on words to satisfy his urge for constructing images; but now he had found a live model. The person in question was also ready to shed her brightly coloured outer petals one by one, in the hope that her efforts would ultimately bear fruit. Amit's sister Lissy had reportedly commented that Katy had become virtually unrecognisable – in other words, that her appearance now was rather too natural. Katy had instructed her friends to address her as Ketaki, a shameless act for someone like her; as if a woman usually dressed in flimsy Shantipuri saris were to coyly don a blouse and chemise. Amit was known to call her 'Keya' in private. There was also a whispered rumour that while boating on the lake at Nainital, Katy had taken the rudder, while Amit read to her from Robi Thakur's *Journey to Nowhere*. But rumours were not to be trusted. Jatishankar drew the conclusion that Amit's heart was sailing on the high waters of escapism.

Ultimately, Amit came back. The city was abuzz with talk of his impending marriage with Katy. But Jati had never heard Amit bring up the subject. Amit's manner had also undergone a marked transformation. He would buy Jati English books as before, but he would not discuss those books with him in the evening, as in earlier times. Jati realised that the discussions had now found a different channel. Nowadays, Amit would not invite Jati to join him for a drive. It was not difficult for someone of Jati's age to sense that there was no room for a third person in Amit's celebration of his own 'journey to nowhere'.

Jati could restrain himself no longer. He accosted Amit and demanded: 'Amitda, you are to marry Miss Katy Mitter, I'm told?'

'Has this reached Labanya's ears?' asked Amit, after a short silence.

'No, I haven't written to her. In the absence of direct confirmation from you, I have said nothing.'

'Your information is correct, but Labanya might misunderstand.'

'Where is the room for misunderstanding?' smiled Jati. 'It's quite straightforward: if you are to marry, then that's exactly what you're going to do.'

'Look, Jati, nothing in human life is ever straightforward. Like the Ganges at its estuary, where it enters the sea, a word to which we affix a single dictionary meaning acquires seven different meanings when it enters the field of real life.'

'In other words, you're saying that the word "marriage" doesn't signify marriage at all?'

'I'm saying that marriage can mean a thousand different things, for it acquires meaning from the way it is practised by human beings. If you try to fathom its meaning without taking human subjects into account, you're bound to be confused.'

'Why don't you explain your own special understanding of its meaning?'

'Definitions are useless. One can only explain with reference to real life. If I say the basic meaning of marriage is love, it leads us to an entirely different issue. As a word, "love" is much more alive than "marriage".'

'In that case, Amitda, we should discard words altogether. Why weigh ourselves down with words as we chase their meaning, if meaning keeps eluding us, sliding this way and that, like a fugitive taking a zigzag route of escape.'

'Well said, my brother! Your association with me has given you a way with words. We need words because we must somehow muddle through in this world. Truths that can't be encompassed by words are discarded because they have no practical value, for words are what we must profess. We have no choice! Even if understanding suffers, words can blindly keep things going.'

'Must we then abandon our subject of discussion?'

'If this discussion is for the sake of knowledge rather than life, then there's no harm in dropping it.'

'Let's assume it's for the sake of life.'

'Bravo! Then listen.'

At this point, there's no harm in inserting a footnote. Of late, Jati had been frequently savouring the tea personally served him by Amit's younger sister Lissy. Perhaps this explained why he harboured no grudge against Amit for discontinuing his evening discourses on literature and their twilight drives in the motor car. He had granted Amit his heartfelt forgiveness.

'Oxygen floats invisibly in the atmosphere, for one of its functions is to sustain life. But it also functions in another way, igniting coal to produce fire, which is essential for many everyday tasks. We can't dismiss either function. Now, do you understand?'

'Not entirely, but I do wish to understand.'

'The love that roams free in the sky is for the companion of one's innermost heart; but the love that permeates all aspects of daily life, is for one's partner in worldly matters. I want both.'

'I'm not sure I understand you correctly. Why not explain a little more clearly, Amitda?'

'Once, I had spread my wings to discover the sky; today, I have found my little nest, where I can fold my wings. But my sky remains, as well.'

'But in you marriage, can partnership and companionship not combine?'

'In life, there could be many opportunities that fail to materialise. Fortunate, indeed, is the man who wins the proverbial prize of half a kingdom plus the princess's hand in marriage. The man who does not enjoy this double advantage is no less fortunate, if by a gift of providence he finds a kingdom in one area of his life and the princess in another.'

'But...'

'But there is a dearth of what you would call romance? Not at all! Must we fall back on story-book stereotypes for our fixed quota of romance? Never! I shall create my own romance. My heavenly romance will remain, and I shall make romance happen on earth, as well. The people you describe as romantic would outlaw the one to preserve the other. They either swim like fish, or roam the earth like cats, or range across the skies like bats. But when it comes to romance, I am like the swan. I have the power to enjoy romance on land, in water, and also in the sky. The river-banks would remain my permanent property; yet, to satisfy my spiritual desires, I would roam the freeways of the sky. Long live my Labanya, long live my Ketaki, and long live Amit Raye in all his dimensions.'

Jati listened in silence, perhaps because the argument did not ring true to his ears.

'Look, my friend,' smiled Amit, observing his expression. 'All words don't apply to everyone. Perhaps I speak only for myself. If you apply my words to yourself, you are bound to misunderstand, and to curse me. All the violence and bloodshed in this world stems from the attempt to impose one person's meanings upon the words of another. Let me give you my point of view in no uncertain terms. I must speak figuratively, or else such ideas would lose their beauty, for the words would feel constrained. My initial relationship with Ketaki was indeed based on love, but it was like water in a pitcher, to be collected daily, and used up everyday. While my love for Labanya remains a lake, its waters not to be carried home, but meant for my consciousness to swim in.'

'But Amitda, must one not choose between the two?' asked Jati, rather awkwardly.

'That may apply to others, but not to me.'

'But if Miss Ketaki were to…'

'She knows everything. Whether she understands everything, I can't say. But I shall devote my entire life to making her understand that I am not deceiving her in any way. She must also realise that she is indebted to Labanya.'

'That's as may be, but it's necessary to inform Labanya of your wedding plans.'

'I shall certainly inform her. But before that, I wish to send her a letter: would you deliver it?'

'I shall.'

Amit wrote:

The other evening, when I stopped at the end of the road, I concluded my journey with a poem. Today, too, I have halted at the end of a journey. I wish to bequeath a poem to this final moment. It will not bear the weight of any other words. The unfortunate Nibaran Chakrabarti died as soon as he was caught out – just like a delicate freshwater fish. Hence I have no choice but to place upon your favourite poet the responsibility of communicating my last thoughts to you.

I glimpse your image eternal, as you vanish
Forever into the secret chamber of my heart.
*   The philosopher's stone, its golden touch, are mine;*
You have filled the spaces of my emptiness.
I found you when my life grew dark; your gift,
The lamp in my heart's shrine.
*   Love emerged from parting's sacred fire,*
In the shape of a prayer, revealed in the glow of sorrow.

Mita

Time passed. One day, Ketaki went to attend the *annaprasan* – the rice-tasting ceremony – of her sister's infant daughter. Amit did not accompany her. As he lay reading the letters of William James, reclining on an armchair with his feet propped up on a stool, Jatishankar brought him a letter from Labanya. One page bore an announcement of Shobhanlal's marriage to Labanya. The wedding was to take place six months later, in the month of Jaishtha, on the crest of the Ramgarh Mountain. On the second page was written:

Do you hear the chariot wheels of Time?
      Ever-unseen, rousing
    The pulse-beats of the universe;
Crushing the heart of darkness, as the stars lament.
        O my friend!
      Time, rushing by,
    Caught me in its net,
      Prisoner of the speeding chariot,
    On a dangerous journey, carried
      Far away from you.
        It seems to me I crossed
      A thousand deaths to reach
The pinnacle of this new dawn –
    My old name tossed to the winds
        By the chariot's rushing speed.
    There is no way back;
      If you gaze at me from afar,
        You will not recognise me.
        My friend, farewell.

Sometime, when you are at ease,
When from the shores of the past,
The night-wind sighs, in the spring breeze,
The sky steeped in tears of fallen bakul flowers,
Seek me then, in the corners of your heart,
For traces left behind. In the twilight of forgetting,
Perhaps a glimmer of light will be seen,
The nameless image of a dream.
And yet it is no dream,
For my love, to me, is the truest thing,
Death-defying,
My eternal prayer-offering, which to you
I bequeath.
I float away on a tide of change
In the journey of time.
My friend, farewell.

Nothing have you lost.
Of mortal clay I'm made; if you saw in me
An image eternal, then let it be
Worshipped at dusk,
Your prayer-game unsullied
By the bleakness of my mundane touch,
Prayer-flowers untainted
By the yearnings of desire.
At your soul's celebration, in vessels meant
To receive emotion's nectar, to quench
Your thirst for words, I shall not mingle
My offering of dust, soaked in my tears.
Today, too, perhaps,
You will create from memory

A dream-image of me, in words inscribed,
Free of burden, free of any claims.
        My friend, farewell.

        Grieve not for me.
For me, there is duty, for me the universe.
        My cup of life is not empty;
To fill the void will ever be my pledge.
If there is one who awaits me eagerly,
        My glory resides in him.
        He who can wrest the fragrant tuberose
        From moonlit nights
                To adorn his prayer offering
        On a dark, moonless night;
        Who can view with mercy infinite
                All that is good and bad in me,
To him I sacrifice my soul

                What I have given you
                Is yours forever.
                Drop by drop I'll now dispense myself;
The piteous moments drink their fill
                As I pour out my heart's oblation.
        O incomparable one!
        O wealthy one!
All that I gave you was really your gift to me;
        For all that you received, you hold me in debt.
                My friend, farewell.

                                        Banya

Notes

1. E.P. Thompson, *Alien Homage: Edward Thompson and Rabindranath Tagore* (Delhi: Oxford University Press, 1993) p.56.

2. Nirad C. Chaudhuri, *Thy Hand, Great Anarch!* (London: Chatto and Windus, 1987) p.608.

3. See *Selected Letters of Rabindranath Tagore*. Translated from Bengali into English, ed. Krishna Dutta and Andrew Robinson (Cambridge: Cambridge University Press, 1997) p.368.

4. Nirad C. Chaudhuri pp.608–10.

5. See *Rabindranath Tagore: Selected Writings on Literature and Language*, ed. Sisir Kumar Das and Sukanta Chaudhuri (New Delhi: Oxford University Press, 2001) p.329.

6. Translated by Jayanti Chattopadhyay, from *Achintya Kumarer Samagra Kabita* (Kolkata, 1974) p.69; cited in Chattopadhyay '*Ghare Baire* and its Readings,' *Rabindranath Tagore's* The Home and the World: *A Critical Companion*, ed. P.K. Datta (Delhi: Permanent Black, 2003) p.197.

7. Nirad C. Chaudhuri p.607.

8. Sankha Ghosh, *Nirman Ar Srishti* (Santiniketan: Visva-Bharati, 1982) pp.100–135.

9. Buddhadeva Basu, *Rabindranath: Kathasahitya* (Kolkata: New Age, 1955) p.125–6. Translation Radha Chakravarty.

10. Nirmal Kumari Mahalanobis, *Kabir Sange Dakshinatye* (Kolkata: Mitra and Ghosh, 1956) pp.89–92.

11. Prasanta Pal, *Rabijibani, Saptam Khanda [Vol. VII], 1321–1326, 1914–1920* (Kolkata: Ananda Publishers, 1997)7. Cited in Datta p.25; Datta's translation.

12. See Das and Chaudhuri pp.185–6.

13. Amartya Sen, 'Tagore and his India', *The New York Review of Books* 44:11 (June 26, 1997).

14. See Krishna Kripalani, *Rabindranath Tagore: A Biography* (Santiniketan: Visva Bharati, 1980) pp.132–3.

15. Dipesh Chakrabarty, 'Witness to Suffering: Domestic Cruelty and the Birth of the Modern Subject in Bengal', *Questions of Modernity*, ed. Timothy Mitchell (Minneapolis: University of Minnesota Press, 2000), pp.49–86. Chakrabarty argues that, in narratives of European bourgeois modernity, the split selves – familial and public – of 'the unitary-expressive and rights-bearing bourgeois subject' would eventually be aligned with each other in a structure of 'repression'. Though influenced by European models, the evolution of the Bengali modern subject did not follow the

same trajectory, for the two axes of subjectivity, the social-public and the familial-private, 'remain much less aligned with each other' (p.77).

16. Chakrabarty 77.

17. Tagore, 'Construction Versus Creation' (1920), *The English Writings of Rabindranath Tagore. Vol. 3: A Miscellany*, ed. Sisir Kumar Das (New Delhi: Sahitya Akademi, 1996) pp.401–409.

18. See Das, ed., *English Writings of Tagore* p.617.

19. Supriya Chaudhuri, 'A Sentimental Education: Love and Marriage in *The Home and the World*', Datta pp.45–65.

20. 'Modern Poetry', Das and Chaudhuri 282.

21. For a detailed calculation of the time-period in which the novel's action is set, see Bhudev Choudhury, *Rabindra Upanyas: Itihaser Prekshite* (Kolkata: Dey's Publishing, 1984) pp.101–102.

22. See Partha Chatterjee, 'The Nationalist Resolution of the Women's Question', in *Recasting Women: Essays in Colonial History*, eds. Kumkum Sangari and Sudesh Vaid (Delhi: Kali for Women, 1989) pp.233–53.

23. Tanika Sarkar, in *Hindu Wife, Hindu Nation: Community, Religion and Cultural Nationalism* (Delhi: Permanent Black, 2001), argues that conjugal marriage was a way for the Bengali Babu to introduce an element of romance or 'prem' into an arranged marriage, as a mode of self-fulfillment in the private realm that would compensate for the ignominy and emasculation he had to suffer under British rule in the public sphere. However, Sarkar also points out the tensions that arose when the idea of companionate marriage was transplanted from the nuclear family of the West into the larger structures of the Indian family.

24. Ketaki Kushari Dyson sees in this an autobiographical element, a bifurcation of Victoria Ocampo's personal traits in Tagore's representations of Labanya and Katy Mitter. See Dyson, *In Your Blossoming Flower-Garden: Rabindranath Tagore and Victoria Ocampo* (New Delhi: Sahitya Akademi, 1961).

Glossary

Abani Thakur: Abanindranath Tagore (1871–51), often regarded as the father of modern Indian painting.

Agrahayan: The eighth month of the Bengali calendar.

Aja: The son of Dilipa and father of Dasharatha in the *Ramayana*. On his way to Indumati's swayamvara, he killed an elephant, liberating a Gandharva who had been under a curse. The grateful Gandharva offered him a quiver full of magic arrows, which helped Aja to win the tournament and the hand of the princess.

Amaravati: The capital city of Indra's celestial kingdom.

Annapurna: Goddess of bounty, associated with rice as daily food. Another name for Parvati, consort of Shiva, who went from home to home collecting rice to appease Shiva's hunger when he came to her as a mendicant priest.

Ashadh: The third month of the Bengali calendar, associated with the monsoon.

Ashtami: Eighth day of the lunar month, here associated with the Durga Puja.

Avantika: Ancient name for the Malwa region in central India, which had Ujjain as its capital; associated with Kalidasa.

Bakul: Fragrant white flower of a large evergreen tree.

Bankim: Bankimchandra Chaterji (1838–94), Bengali novelist.

Bhat: A particular mixed caste, traditional singers of panegyrics.

Bhuichampa: The *kaemferia rotunda*, a fragrant flower

Bijoyadashami: The tenth day of the light half of the month of Ashwin, when the image of Durga is ritually immersed at the end of the Durga Puja.

Brahma: The god of creation, first of the triad of leading Hindu deities.

Brahmins: Members of the priestly caste.

Chandimandap: Shrine for the worship of Durga.

Chandra: The moon as deity.

Dakshayajna: Daksha, born from Brahma's right thumb, was the father of Sati and father-in-law of Shiva. He performed a sacrifice, where Shiva was publicly abused when he arrived uninvited. Shiva ruined the ceremony and killed Daksha in a fury.

Damayanti: Daughter of King Bhima of Vidarbha, she wishes to marry the handsome King Nala, who sends a beautiful bird to tell her of his secret love for her. At her *swayamvara*, various deities vie for her hand, but she chooses Nala for her husband. The Mahabharata narrates the legend of Damayanti's loyalty and devotion to Nala, through the trials and tribulations that follow.

Dhanpati: A wealthy merchant who falls in love with his sister-in-law Khullana and marries her, only to be unfaithful to her afterwards. The *Chandimangal* describes Dhanpati's travels, his capture and imprisonment, and eventual release, accomplished by Khullana's son Sriman with the aid of the goddess Chandi.

Durga: Goddess, consort of Shiva, who slew the demon Mahishasura.

Gita: A long poem of 700 verses in the Mahabharata, containing Krishna's advice to Arjuna on the battlefield.

Gupta Kingdom: The Gupta dynasty ruled India *c*.AD 320–540.

Hanuman: The monkey god, ally of Rama, in the *Ramayana*.

Hari: Another name for Krishna.

Indra: King of the Hindu pantheon of deities.

Indumati: Princess of Vidarbha, who chose Prince Aja to be her husband at her *swayamvara*. She died when a multitude of flowers smothered her while she was asleep in her orchard.

Jatayu: The giant bird who tries to rescue Sita from the clutches of Ravana in the *Ramayana*.

Jhaptaal: A ten-beat rhythm cycle in Hindustani classical music.

Kanak-champa: Fragrant, gold-coloured flower.

Kishkindhya: Capital of the monkey kingdom in the *Ramayana*.

Krisnachaturdashi: Fourteenth day of the lunar fortnight, when the moon is in the dark quarter.

Lakshmi: Goddess of wealth and prosperity.

Malavika: Kalidasa's *Malavikaagnimitra* describes the love of Agnimitra of Vidisha, King of the Shungas, for Malavika, the beautiful handmaiden of his chief queen.

Manasarovar: A lake in the Himalayas, associated with the mythical bird, the Paramhamsa.

Mandar mountain: The mountain that was used by the deities and demons to churn the ocean for nectar.

Meghdoot: Kalidasa's *Meghadutam* is a poem of 115 stanzas, in which a *yaksha* or demigod, banished to Ramagiri in Central India, uses a cloud as messenger to send an amorous message to his wife in the Himalayan town called Alaka.

Meghnad: Michael Madhusudan Dutt's *Meghnadbadh Kavya* depicts the slaying of Meghnad, son of Ravana in the Ramayana.

Narad: A sage who fomented discord among gods and men.

Padavali: Series of verses, usually associated with the Vaishnava tradition.

Papad: Thin, crisp snack made from spiced pulses.

Paramhamsa: Mythical swan, believed to float on the lake Manasarovar in the Himalayas. Also the name of Ramakrishna, the philosopher-saint.

Poush festival: Celebrations held during Paush, the ninth month of the Bengali calendar.

Pitha: A snack, usually made from ground rice.

Radha: Consort of Krishna.

Raghuvamsha: Kalidasa's poem narrates the history of the family of Rama from its earliest antecedents, including the principal events of Valmiki's *Ramayana*.

Ravana: Rama's adversary, the demon king of Lanka, who abducts Sita in the *Ramayana*.

Sati: The daughter of Daksha and wife of Shiva; she was killed, and her body dismembered, by an enraged Shiva in his dance of destruction, after he was humiliated at Daksha's sacrificial ceremony.

Shakuntala: In Kalidasa's *Abhijnanashakuntalam*, King Dushyanta marries Shakuntala, foster daughter of sage Kanva. Cursed by sage Durvasha, Dushyanta forgets Shakuntala. His memory is restored when a ring, his token of remembrance to her, is found inside the belly of a fish.

Shiva: The third deity of the Hindu triad.

Sita: Wife of Lord Rama in the *Ramayana*.

Srijukta: Honorific prefix to the names of men; also means 'person of grace and eminence'.

Srimati: Appellation prefixed before the names of women; also means 'person of grace and beauty'.

Stupa: Buddhist monument, thought to enshrine the relics of the Buddha.

Uma: Another name for Parvati, consort of Shiva. She underwent terrible forms of asceticism to win Shiva.

Vaidya: An upper-class Hindu caste; considered a mixed caste.

Varun: God of the sea.

Vidyapati: Vaishnava poet (1374–1460), best known for his erotic poems in Maithili, depicting the love of Radha and Krishna.

Vishnu: Second of the triad of Hindu deities, regarded as the preserver

Biographical note

Rabindranath Tagore was born in May 1861 in Calcutta. He was the youngest of thirteen surviving children. His father Debendranath Tagore was a leader of the Brahmo Samaj, which was a new religious sect in nineteenth-century Bengal. Having turned eleven, 'Rabi' was taken on a tour of India, culminating in Dalhousie where he was to be immersed in literature and culture.

Previously for the most part educated at home, but aiming to become a barrister, at seventeen Tagore enrolled in a Brighton public school and subsequently studied law at University College London. He left, however, without a degree and returned to Bengal in 1880. His marriage to Mrinalini Devi resulted in five children, two of whom died in childhood. In 1890, Tagore took over the management of his family's estates. This was a very fruitful time for Tagore, in which he wrote seven volumes of poetry.

In 1901, Tagore moved to Santiniketan to found an ashram. Throughout his life, Tagore was to remain heavily involved in all aspects of Santiniketan. In particular the school, fundraising and teaching were his priorities. It was during this period of his life that Tagore was to lose two of his children and his wife.

Successful and prolific in all genres of literature, Tagore was primarily a poet. Championed in the West by such figures as W.B. Yeats, Tagore was awarded the Nobel Prize for Literature in 1913, following the publication of *Gitanjali* in 1912. Tagore also wrote eight novels and four novellas. His writings display engagements with wide-ranging themes, from nationalism, identity and personal freedom to family life.

Tagore's work also includes musical dramas, dance dramas, essays of all types, travel diaries, and two autobiographies, the last shortly before his death. Tagore also left numerous drawings and paintings, and songs for which he wrote the music himself. Two of Tagore's songs, part of an output of more than 2,000, became the national anthems of India and Bangladesh.

Tagore was knighted in 1915, but renounced the title in 1919 in protest over the Jallianwala Bagh massacre. His last years were marred by severe illness which resulted on several occasions in him losing consciousness and falling into a coma for extended periods of time. Tagore died, in August 1941, in the Joradsanko mansion in which he had been brought up.